THE TRIUMVIRATE ANTHOLOGY

A Quarterly of Science Fiction, Fantasy, & Horror. Volume Two

DAVID OLIVER KLING PRESENTS

CONTENTS

EDITORIAL

By David Oliver Kling

Being in my 50s with a toddler is an amazing experience. My daughter will be five in October 2022, and she is growing up quickly. It seems just yesterday that she was born. When she was born, I spent a lot of time in the hospital cafeteria. While in the cafeteria, I became friends with one of the cooks. This was back in 2017. I discovered this cook was also an artist, and I ended up commissioning him to do an illustration of my wife and I holding our newborn while dressed as Starfleet officers from Star Trek, of course he depicted us as Vulcans. As I write this, I cast my gaze onto my wall and see the five family illustrations I have commissioned this artist. Near Vivianne's first birthday we commissioned the family in a Star Wars setting, I was Darth Vader without the helmet and Vivianne was my Sith apprentice with Jacki, my wife, dressed as a Jedi looking at us like, "Good grief!" Year three saw us again as Starfleet officers but this time Vivianne is playing with a pile of tribbles. Year four saw us in a glamor shot like pose as Borg from Star Trek, this is my favorite of all! The most recent illustration has a Frozen theme. Since Vivianne longs to become a princess, we depicted her as Elsa from Frozen and my wife and I as Anna and Kristoff. I am not sure what we will have done this year. Vivianne has been obsessed with the Wizard of Oz, so maybe we will go with an Oz theme. With The Orville season three out this year, maybe we will go with an Orville theme? My negotiations with Jacki may take a while.

My daughter, Vivianne, has become my "muse." I told my wife recently that I seek to build a legacy. After I am gone, I want to leave something for others to enjoy. I work in hospice as a chaplain and have been in this line of work since 2013. I have lost between ten and thirty patients each month. You do the math, that is a lot of people who I have known and who have died. Seeing all this death, I am ever mindful of what is left behind. I want my daughter, in her old age, to look back at her father's work and be proud. So, I keep plugging away on this and other projects.

I have always had a "do it yourself" spirit. If I don't know how to do something, I will watch as many YouTube videos, and read as many books, as necessary to master what I need to know. Fortunately, I have no interest in brain surgery, but I learned how to host and produce a podcast, and to publish content on both YouTube and print and digital media by both trial and error and watching videos and reading. It's a safe assumption that about half of the media content I consume is "independently" produced content. I say half because I watch a lot of television because there is so much superb content out there; people like me and not lavish corporations with lots of money and an enormous staff of producers. People like me produced all the podcasts I consume. Likewise, the YouTube content I watch are independently produced. And, the YouTube content I watch is independently produced. When I was young, in the 1980s, I read a lot of comics but tended towards the independent market back then too. I used to read comics produced by the "little guys," such titles as Justice Machine, Elementals, and Teenage Mutant Ninja Turtles (before they were massively popular).

With technology being what it is today, the world is now ripe for independent content producers to be seen, and their work enjoyed. Ideas, stories, and concepts are proliferating because the barrier to entry has become easier. I have even listened to several audio books produced by independent publishers. We live in a world where great content is available on many platforms giving voice to people who would never have been given a voice. There is a lot about the 1980s of my youth that I miss and look upon fondly. I value the world of opportunity that we live in today and look forward to creating a legacy that my daughter Vivianne can be proud of her dad.

CHAPTER ONE

"MERCHANT OF DEATH"

BY NICHOLAS MACON HURST

"HUMANS ARE A PECULIAR race. I'd heard of them before, a loose group of aliens in an uncharted region of the galaxy. One of their many nations had managed to defeat the Rai'Kavosh, which in itself is a monumental achievement. Overnight, those young upstarts made waves, though not for the reasons you might think. You see, most of us, we knew better. No one beats the Rai'Kavosh. No one has the firepower or the numbers. Or so I thought. But one human, a simple peddler, proved me wrong.

"I'm a Moltarian, from the Moltarian Confederacy. We control three systems full of resources, filled to the brim with our kind. Sure, sounds like a lot until you look at our history and realize that until ten human years ago, we controlled fifteen. Blame the Cordov. They had bled their space dry and were looking for more, deciding the Confederacy had what they wanted. They pushed us back, hard, before we even knew they were coming. They took three systems before the

Council got wind of the invasion. The Fleet tried their best, but we're an isolated people. We only had so much territory because no one paid us any mind, meaning we had very little experience fighting a war.

Not that most people would, with the Rai'Kavosh and the Oro Convent around. Before long, refugees were flooding the inner systems and Trade Station 47, my station, became a temporary housing area for refugees waiting on a permanent shelter on the surface of the planet. We knew they were coming and we were hoping they'd leave the station unmolested, seeing as there was nothing to gain from its destruction. Nonetheless, we were absolutely terrified, stalk eyes clacking in worry when the hyperfootprint appeared on our scanners, one large enough to be a Cordov Superbattleship. But it wasn't. It was a single ship of unknown design, loudly broadcasting a message we couldn't translate, but we didn't detect a weapons signature, so we cautiously sent them coordinates to a docking bay.

"The strangers didn't speak our language, which was normal, but we Moltarians have a fallback: our telepathy. Shame you can't send telepathic messages over comms, someone should really work on that. Or get the Domeosapians to give up their tech. Apologies, getting sidetracked. Anyway, the first person to disembark the ship was a short alien, about 162 centimeters, ⅔ the size of an adult Moltarian. They didn't even flinch when I spoke to their mind, which told me they'd been exposed to telepathy before.

Apparently, this was a human, a woman calling herself Josefina Perez, a freighter captain from a place called Mexico. I later learned it was a place on the human homeworld of Earth. She said she was technically making First Contact, but really just looking for a place to maybe take on some goods to sell at home and give her crew some rest, and this Seedy Joint was perfect. We didn't exactly have the space, due to the refugees, but a Stationmaster never says no to business on their station, so of course I said yes.

Her ship, a Queen Celeste-class Freighter, had a crew of only 20 other humans, which struck me as odd. Her ship was massive, a full kilometer (a human measurement) in length, and should have had room for three times that, plus the cargo space. But she waved me off when I questioned her. Instead, she wanted to know all about my people, saying that her leader (something called an Emperor) would love to deal with us. I had my doubts, but whatever.

"In my office, which had a small window overlooking the sparsely populated planet below, we exchanged stories. She was from the main nation, the ones that claimed a victory over the Rai'Kavosh. She called it the Solarian Empire, saying it was the oldest human nation in space and held their homeworld as a capital. Until humanity, the idea of multiple different nations of the same species made no sense, but as I said, humans are a peculiar people. I told her about the Confederacy and she seemed interested, even asking for mundane specifics, mostly about culture and religion. I told her about Erlah, the place where those who have brought harm upon others are sent, dragged down by demons. She countered with a place called Hell, where a servant of her god was cast out with his followers for their rebellion and the souls of humans that refused to accept the message of her god were sent to be tortured for all eternity, as well as those that took their own lives, and a myriad of other reasons. It was a horrible place by the sound of it and I was honestly disgusted by it, even with the notion of paradise for the faithful. She seemed to notice my distress, unusual for a race that we just met, so she talked about her past. Three spawn-mates, one male, two females, and all of them joined their nation's military, though while all her spawn mates, which she called siblings, went into the ground forces, she chose the Fleet. Or, as she stressed, the Solarian Navy. A fleet is a formation in human terms.

Either way, it struck my interest, so I asked about her experience. She told me tales of pirate hunting, peacekeeping and the one that really got my attention, was a story of a border clash with another human nation back when she commanded what she called a light cruiser before she retired and bought her current ship, CMV Gabriel the Messenger. Now, there was this standing order that we don't discuss current events with aliens, especially ones that might put us in a bad light, but I felt there was no harm in it. I started telling her about the Cordov and their inevitable encroaching on our homeworld. Had I known humans as well as I did, I wouldn't have gone into much detail, but I was inexperienced with her kind and didn't know what the slow change of her face meant. She was warm and smiling when I was talking but by the time I finished, she looked...her face was as hard as the armor of a warship and her eyes could have doubled as targeting for missile batteries. She started asking about defenses and the strength of the fleet, which I was ashamed I couldn't answer. She told me she'd have to talk to her people about this, but I initially brushed it off. She left soon after that, back to her ship.

"Not too long after, station control reported she sent a burst transmission off into the void without having reported her intentions. This was a breach of conduct, as transmissions tended to alert the Cordov, but she was a guest and a new one at that. She didn't know any better. The next cycle, her crew began unloading containers from her freighter, which turned out to be supplies. Cloth that could be used to cover one's body, food that humans eat, water, and various luxury items that could be sold for a decent amount. I told her that she wouldn't find much business here, at least not for the price some of her stuff would fetch due to refugees, but she waved me off. She said these were donations. Humans had a policy of helping those in need. Humanitarian aid, she called it. Fitting that a term meant to provide assistance had their name in it. The refugees usually would have swarmed the workers, but she kept them at bay with firm words and rather judicious waving around of what she called a baseball bat. Once the crowd was under control, they began passing out supplies, though warning that the food was meant for humans and couldn't be guaranteed safe.

Luckily, it wasn't too far off, though I heard it caused many a digestive issue. It was a great help and eased the stress on station logistics. Perez informed me that she'd called her people, specifically her Navy, and had told them of the situation. Even if Shield Base, I'm guessing the command station of her Navy, didn't want to get involved in our war, they'd still send more aid. In fact, she guaranteed that there'd be supply ships coming. When I told her the Cordov had attacked supply ships in the past, she laughed, telling me that if the Cordov could get past the escorts, they deserve the kill. Humans have a bit of an egotistical streak, it seemed. She did, however, make a single trade. She traded me all of the supplies for a translation program. Apparently, her people could make one quickly, if they had a database of our language. I was glad to provide it and two of her people vanished into the ship and never came back out, supposedly to get to work.

"Two cycles later, the fateful day came. I was called to Station Control as a large hyperfootprint was detected. The Cordov Armada had finally arrived and were heading into the system. It was the majority of their force, 30 ships in all, led by their two Superbattleships. This wasn't a raiding party, this was a force meant to conquer and destroy. When we broadcast our non-combatant status, we were promptly ignored and detected shields being raised. Trade Station 47 had no weapons and only basic shielding to protect from debris, so the Armada would be making quick work of us. As I prepared myself for the Ritual of Death, as I knew the refugees were, I received a strange message. CMV Gabriel the Messenger was requesting permission to depart. I granted it, waiving the docking fees, as I knew a freighter would be just as vulnerable if it stayed and the last thing her Empire needed was to be dragged into our war. With the stories she told me about border clashes and piracy, they must've had so few ships to spare. To my surprise, however, the ship was on an intercept course for the approaching Armada, the massive ship burning away at a speed it shouldn't have been able to achieve. I commed Perez to ask what she was doing, now that her translation program was up and running, and she told me that she couldn't sit back and just watch as unarmed innocents were slaughtered. It was against her moral and religious code and was against the oath she took when she joined the Solarian Navy, and that oath demanded she protect this seedy joint. When I reminded her that she, too, was an unarmed innocent, she only laughed. She told me that that was the point. Before she cut the line, I heard her order the Spanish Inquisition, though at the time, the term was meaningless to me.

"As the freighter approached, the Armada ignored it. Excuse me, I forgot humans refer to their ships as she. They must have thought she was harmless as they waited for her to come into range. The human ship may have been as large as the Superbattleships, but the translation program allowed them to broadcast their status as a freighter. She moved past their screening units unscathed as the Superbattleship's plasma cannons began charging. No matter how powerful her shields may be, a Cordov Superbattleship's main guns were powerful enough to slag a warship's armor. I watched in horror as I saw the suicidal range she was at. At that range, the Cordov could have thrown rocks and hit the ship. And then, there was a massive surge of energy before the Superbattleship shuddered like a wounded animal. I was in shock as the energy surge had come from the human freighter. We detected it again and the Superbattleship began venting atmosphere as the other ships around finally realized something was up. As Gabriel began to turn, through the interference, I finally picked it up. The human freighter was running energy weapons, though at a size vastly smaller than anything the Cordov had ever managed to achieve. Explosions at the sides of the freighter made my hearts skip a beat until I realized she'd fired missiles, now streaking toward the light ships. Cordov missile defense was impressive, with rarely a missile getting a hit in. so, imagine my surprise when the missiles all detonated before impact, just out of range of Cordov plasma missile defenses and more energy surges were picked up. The humans were firing missiles that themselves fired small energy weapons. The lasers ripped through the unprepared ships, killing all but one, which started to limp away before three more missiles ran it down. And then their luck changed.

"The entire Armada had changed their plans and decided to focus their entire fury on this one ship, though by now, we could all pick up the impressive array of weaponry aboard. I suddenly realized why there was so little room as we counted, on each side, five energy weapons, five plasma weapons per side, three launchers, and a single mass driver. As the enemy opened fire, the shields flared, actually taking the brunt of the damage as more missiles streaked away from the ship. The injured Superbattleship was hit with a pair of kinetic rounds, shattering the shields seconds before plasma bolts slammed into the armor, adding to the hellacious damage the first two energy barrages dealt. Everyone knew kinetics were the perfect counter to shields, but the size of the weapon, plus the ammo requirements, meant few fleets used them. As we watched, mesmerized by the back and forth, my mind turned back to my first conversation with Perez, when she mentioned her religion's Hell. I made up my mind that her crew had to be escaped followers of the rebellious servant, because not once did the weapons on Gabriel slow their rate of fire. You could accurately time the reload speed of the missiles and mass drivers as they fired with a precision that no Moltarian could have matched under that much enemy fire. And there was a lot of it. As powerful as the human's first attacks had been, the element of surprise was lost and that ship was too large to be able to avoid all the plasma and missiles thrown their way. But they still fought on. More and more Cordov ships fell, but we began noticing less fire from Gabriel. I finally worked up the nerve to comm the ship and Perez answered. She was a mess, her hair frazzled, a red substance on her face I learned later to be their blood. But her eyes had a fire in them and she was grinning like her mind had left her. I told her to leave, she'd done enough and didn't need to sacrifice her crew, but she told me something in a language I later learned to be Spanish. The only word I remember is mother. She sent another burst transmission to the station, encrypted, and asked me to give it to her people. I told her to give it to them herself, but she shook her head, saying that her weapons were already glitching and that she had enough power left to fire the hyperdrive. I told her not to, that her religion says that she'll go straight to Hell. The last words I ever heard from her was telling me that someone had to drag these bastards to Erlah.

"CMV Gabriel the Messenger fired her hyperdrive and, knowing what I do about astrogation, had disabled all the safeties and set the destination as the exact point they were at. The freighter ripped open the fabric of space, bleeding the radiation of hyperspace into normal space as the detonation engulfed the majority of the light ships around her, making a final shipment of death to the enemy. When the hyperblindess that inflicted on us had faded, my hearts fell. For all her sacrifice, for all her hard work, one of the Superbattleships remained, as well as three of her screen. But they were slower. Either she'd cowed them...or she'd damaged their engines. It didn't matter either way, as the Cordov were approaching still. They would be in range in a quarter of a cycle, but it was far longer than we'd expected. It gave us enough time to try and come up with a lottery on who we could evacuate on the few sub-light shuttles, so the refugees could die on the surface of a planet, instead of suffocating in vacuum.

"They were in range by the time we had the two shuttles loaded up. I'd stood on the observation deck, facing the approaching enemy. I had decided that I would be the first to die, at least symbolically. I closed my eyes as I waited for death...which never came. They should have fired by now. But before I could theorize as to why they hadn't fired, an excited voice came over the comm from the young technician still in Station Control. Another hyperfootprint had been detected. When I pulled up the feed, I had to demand the technician check the sensors for damage, but he reported that the sensors were undamaged. 350 ships, ranging from 375 meters to six behemoth ships over five kilometers in length, had entered the system with an unknown IFF tag. 350 ships was larger than the Confederate Fleet and the Cordov Armada combined. But it was the transmission that told me all I needed to know. A visual feed was established, revealing a human man in a red uniform with a face that matched Perez's back when I told her our situation. He announced himself as Rear Admiral Keegan Hines, the commanding officer of Task Group 32.7 of the Solarian Navy on a relief mission, and that the system was under their control. The Cordov mustn't have understood a single word, but you'd have to be an idiot not to recognize superior firepower and a willingness to use it. But I also never said the Cordov were smart. They turned their weapons to the new arrivals, but never got a shot off as the humans opened fire, turning the remaining four ships into free floating atoms before Cortez asked me who was in charge and for a status report. I've never been so happy in my life to see an alien."

The avian-looking Moltarian with stalk eyes and three legs in a tripod arrangement finally finished his story, the fine hair on his chest has puffed up with emotion, the Moltarian equivalent of holding back tears. He stood before a thick desk that separated him from a man in a simple lavender suit, stroking his beard, long hair brown tumbling down his shoulders. The Stationmaster of Trade Station 47 had completed the final request of Josefina Perez, delivering her encrypted message to her people. However, he didn't expect that Emperor Rudolph I would want to hear the events of the Battle of Curle IV personally.

"Stationmaster Magravach, was it? I appreciate you coming to tell me this personally. I had my theories when Admiral Northe told me one of his reserve officers had made contact and was demanding assistance, but nothing of this magnitude. While you were traveling here, I sent a message to your Council. The Solarian Empire will send, free of charge, any aid needed to alleviate the effects of a war of aggression. I've also informed the Cordov that under no circumstances are they to enter your space, as my ships have orders to use lethal force. Task Force Orion has been dispatched to begin to retake your lost systems and a team from the Minister of Foreign Affairs is on their way to your capital to discuss terms of a treaty."

A week ago, Magravach would have been absolutely floored at the amount of diplomatic and military power these humans had to casually swing about, but at this point, nothing surprised him.

"Your Majesty, you said you had theories, may I ask what they were?"

Rudolph smiled and reached under the desk before standing up, holding a box and a bundle of cloth in his hands.

"They were about how a run in with the Cordov would have gone. And I was not let down. And since Captain Perez deemed it necessary to show the Cordov what humanity does to its enemies, it's my turn to show the Moltarian Confederacy how we treat our heroes."

He set the bundle on the table and opened the box.

"The Imperial Medal of Heroism. The Imperial Senate has it awarded to any member of the Solarian military that displays gallantry, courage, and self-sacrifice above and beyond the call of duty. Though Captain Perez was a reserve officer and technically off duty and in her private Armed Merchant Cruiser, she had no oath or duty to defend your people, nor was she under orders. But she did. And so, the Senate deemed it a worthy enough cause to bend the rules and award her this. And, as for the other..."

Rudolph carefully unwrapped the bundle of cloth, revealing a ceremonial sword in a gilded scabbard. The Stationmaster gave the Emperor a curious look, but held his beak. He'd learned swiftly the human leader liked to teach.

"The Order of Gunther is something I personally give to those that I feel have performed a great service for the Solarian Empire or for humanity as a whole. However, today, I am expanding the Order. Because the galaxy is getting larger, I can no longer, in good conscience, not recognize those that sacrifice for those not of their own kind. And so, I, Rudolph Gerhardt Gunther, Emperor Rudolph I of the Solarian Empire, posthumously inducted Josefina Perez into the Order with the rank of Knight-Captain."

He sat on the desk, next to the two awards, as the Moltarian processed everything.

"Your Majesty," he started to ask, choosing his words carefully, "my people have similar things we can award. But, if I may ask, why are you presenting this to me as if I am receiving it?"

Rudolph couldn't help but grin as the alien walked right into his carefully laid trap.

"Because you are. You see, Captain Perez didn't tell you the whole story. Her siblings all died in the Rai'Kavosh Incursion. Her parents died long ago. She had no one but her crew. And, as of a week and a half ago, you and your people. So, by tradition, the awards are given to your people to safeguard. Perez was human, yes, but through her actions, she became a Moltarian, at least in spirit. Yes, I did some research on your religion as you traveled. And I also spoke with the Pope, the man at the head of her religion. While Perez did, in fact, take her own life, she did so to save the lives of others while in defense of the innocent. She isn't being punished, as you probably worried, but instead in her paradise. So, take the Medal, take the sword, and bring them home. Perez's body is gone, but you now have physical mementos."

Magravach could only nod, the feeling in his hearts making it hard to breathe. And as he returned home, he decided that Perez's Medal would go to the Council for display on the new monument they were erecting, but her sword would go to the station. When he set foot in the docking bay, he was greeted by a mural of Perez and her crew, faces in defiant smiles, looking right at anyone that stepped onto the station. A warning to those that looked upon them, that the Merchant of Death would not take kindly to those that would threaten Perez's Seedy Joint.

CHAPTER TWO

"SEEKING THE STONE"

BY ROB STONE

THE AMBULANCE SCREAMED ITS' sirens, and it was racing up to 70mph. The hospital was not far. The three EMT's did not think the old man would make it. No one knew who he was, he had no ID, they had no idea what medications he took. All he had on him was a keycard and odd jewelry. When they cut away part of his shirt from the stab wound, they found his skin supple like a teenager. It was very odd. The old collarless shirt looked ancient, yet it had no stain, and it was sunburned more than any person could be. They sought to stop the blood. Knowing there was a great deal of internal damage to the sternum, where the knife was still embedded when they arrived, they did not remove it concerned he would bleed out.

Jacob, the primary EMT, had heard part of the story from the officers at the scene. It seems the old man was sitting at a table by himself at a café having a rather large vat of coffee and eating when a few young men began harassing him in some insulting comments. They talked about his rummaged hair and his old clothes, his perceived homelessness, he was a bum they said, probably never worked a day in his life. The old man laughed at them and with whit and small gestures gave what he got. A smaller man in the throng threatened him and when the old man told him to screw off, the thug drew a knife and thrust it into the old man's chest. The officer said when he did, the old man leaned in and kissed him, an odd gesture. The youngsters tried to flee but the police had them in custody.

As the portable x-ray was being used to ascertain the depth of the 9-inch knife through the sternum, the lights began to flicker. On and off like a strobe light, then all at once they all just burst spewing the glass in all directions. Jacob looked down and noticed the old man's eyes were open and were a strange blue color and deep as the ocean. They stared up at him. The explosion of all the bulbs forced the ambulance to stop. Jacob's colleague and the driver all looked to the patient. When Jacob looked back to the wound it was gone. He squinted and looked hard, touched with glove hand and the old man giggled, pushing the hand away. "If you would be so kind," the old man offered him his arm to remove the IV and monitor cables.

Jacob had no idea what to do, he just looked at him, his jaw opened. The second, Kylie, removed the IV and was about to add the cotton and wrap it but when she returned to do that he had pulled back and was smiling at them. He still has a swollen lip from falling after he was stabbed but that was the only visible sign that remained from the incident. "Thank you for your assistance, may I get out here? I no longer need your help," the man said.

All three just looked at each other. The driver, not having seen the instant recovery tried to get the man's name, ID, and a way for him to pay for the ride. His gentle soothing tones as he sat up and expressed his thanks allowed the other two to let him out the back doors. As he descended the step the driver stepped out to assist, he asked the man his name. "What does it matter?" the old fellow asked.

"Look, we picked you up with a stab wound, we drove you halfway to the hospital. You have no ID. You were not conscious. Now there is no wound," he said, looking down at the man's chest.

The patient smiled at him, tapped him on the shoulder and said, "Emrys, my name is Emrys."

With his name in the air, he turned and walked to the sidewalk and then he walked away. With no cell phone, no bags, no identification, he simply walked to the place he stayed. Seven miles later he arrived at his apartment. He walked into the lobby and by the front desk manager who looked concerned that the nice old man in the penthouse had a ripped shirt and had a busted lip. He had learned not to ask though, Emyrs did not like questions.

The old man bowed his head as he walked by, his disposition was the same as usual. He tapped the button for the elevator. Moments later he was rising to his apartment in the penthouse. As the doors opened, he reached for his key, clipped to his belt. He waived himself in and the door released its lock. He clipped the key back and pushed open the door.

The very large open canvas lay before him. It had little furniture, nothing on the walls, and lay bare from the last person who lived there. As Emrys turned the corner a large study was packed rather haphazardly with books, papers, scrolls, and implements of all kinds. A writing desk sat in the corner, very old and filled with papers. He strode by it looking up at the clock and realizing it was just 8AM. He moved to the kitchen, feeling rather hungry. He opened the fridge and a large pot sat waiting for him. He pulled it out and set it on the stove, turning it on. Why it heated he went off to his bedroom.

Here was a bed, unmade and very comfortable, and he turned to the closet walking in and replaced his shirt with a black one which looked the as the ripped one he cast off into the trash. A chest lay in the closet by his feet but there were very little clothes on his side. The other side was a plethora of black woman's clothing. The half full pot was belching forward the green liquid as it began to get close to a boil. Emrys grabbed a wooden spoon and began to stir it. He opened a cabinet. It was filled with spices, herbs, and many tincture bottles. He grabbed this one and that one. He smelled then what he needed to smell, and a singsong entered his throat.

He grabbed a goblet, then he put on the kettle with water. Moments later he was sitting at his writing desk with two cups. The goblet with the green soup like liquid and the other a steeped cup of tea. The voice was still a singsong as he made his way through his papers at his writing desk, mostly newspapers. Under then all around were his own scribblings from a fountain pen which lay before him perched in its holder. The script he used could not have been read by anyone. The language was one he used many years ago, in his youth, even then it did not have a script. It was only verbal, never meant to be written. Emyrs himself made the script into a written language and he had used it ever since.

After reading and writing for some time he heard the door open and close. He said nothing, on his third mug of tea, he sipped and waited to see who would come forth. He heard it first, the clip clap of the heels. He saw her turn towards the bedroom. The beautiful legs and gate as she moved like a cat, expecting him to still be in bed. Her hair was long and just as dark, so dark it had aspects of slate gray. She caught sight of the pot and the tea kettle and turned on her heels peering at him, she smiled. "You are up early, my lord," she said with a little humor, and a lot of sarcasm. "Aye got stabbed at my café last night lass," his thick accent came forward.

"Stabbed, why?" she looked more concerned and came forward, she saw he was fine when she got closer except the lip, she mused, "You smell of it."

Emrys acted as if he was not aware and sipped the tea.

She looked to be in her late 20's, but she was far from it. The long skirt to the knee, tight but not too tight, the blousy top, all black. By her makeup it could be assumed she was a makeup artist, it was flawless. Her pale skin made her look like a Gothic star. Lythe in figure, taunt in body, she was almost frail looking, but her eyes betrayed her. She was a force of nature. Her full and generous eyes carried malice at times and were soaked in sarcasm. She had seen so much and at times they told her tales for her. She was no one's fool. The nails were always done well, this time black with electric aspects of white and silver. A single ring on her ring finger did not look at all like a wedding ring. It was both a wedding ring and is not.

When it was clear her lord was not going to tell his story of the stabbing she turned and walked to the kitchen to get her share of the green soup she ladled into a bowl. Emyrs looked up at her now and again, but he was not distracted. He resumed the work. A flick of a finger and the small piano in the corner of the living room came to life rolling out some Celtic tunes. Without turning the young woman smiled and shook her head. She sniffed the air and could smell it. Magic, real magic has a scent. It is unmistakable. It saturated his blood and she sought to gain it. Many confused magic with being taught but the power was not that easy. Sure, you could learn some conjuring but real sorcery is blood magic, and it had a scent. It is only in the blood one can be a full mage. Her lord was so full of it, it was difficult for him to hold it all in at times.

"Am I to learn anything today my lord?" she asked, now sitting on the edge of the counter with crossed legs, bouncing the top one anxiously. She was eating away at the green mealy liquid that steamed in her face.

"Mm, not today little one, I must learn more about a missing part."

"The gem?"

"Aye, it must be returned."

"Why is it so important to you?"

The old man looked up and smiled at her, "Do not ask questions you know the answer to."

She did not respond, she just kept eating. Then he was on his feet. He grabbed a small cane that looked more like a cudgel from a set of sticks in an umbrella stand, rolled it in his hands and set out. She sat up seeing the look in his eyes.

"Can I join you my lord," she offered.

"Ya' may," he said, crossing the large room much quicker than someone who looked half his age. He grabbed a coat, put it on, reached down for a skull cap to cover his balding scalp. The woman beside him put her leather coat back on, looking stylish beside someone who looked rather basic. They grinned, nodded at one another and were off.

They quickly got to the subway and headed closer to downtown. In the tunnel she tried again at small talk.

"What were you reading in the study?" she asked, wondering where they were going. He hesitated, then leaned into her so he had her ear alone. "The want ads, people still sell things that way. Especially unlawful or stolen things. They are trying to sell what is mine and I must get it back."

The doors opened and they walked up to the streets, now Emrys acted as if he were looking his age and he slowly leaned on the cane and made his way to a rundown apartment building. By now it was past midday with some cloud cover. He made his way to the front of the building and rang the bell.

"Yeah", a man said back through the buzzer.

"Hello young man, I am trying to get to the guy selling the gem in the paper?"

"Uh, yeah that sold already."

"Hm, that is a shame, I was ready to pay three times what you wanted. I can get one somewhere..." but before he could finish the person buzzed him up. Emyrs hurried to catch the door and took the four flights up. When they arrived Emrys acted as if he were catching his breath. His student followed in his wake.

When they reached the top the fellow who buzzed them in was waiting in the door frame, "So, old fella, you said you have the money to pay for it, I might have some other things you might like so I figured since you were here..."

"Your name?" Emrys asked, still sucking for breath.

"Chris, name's Chris, you want to come in?" he offered and then he saw the student and stood up straighter and combed back his crazy hair with his hand.

Chris was living in a flop house and was embarrassed to bring them into his place, but it was too late, and he wondered if he could still unload the money off the old man and sell some of his crap. Chris was a low-class crook, just reselling stolen items. His apartment was a wreck, and it did not smell very good, the student put the back of her hand under her nose smelling her own perfume. They all chatted for a few moments while looking around, but it was clear the old man wanted the gem and nothing else.

"Who did you sell it to?" Emrys asked, leaning on the cane.

"Some guy, I don't know. He paid the $600 and I took it and then he left. He texted me when he saw it in the paper. He just left a few minutes ago."

The old man turned to his student who turned without a word and left out the door quickly and with purpose. Chris noticed two gems on the chest of the old man and knew they were old and expensive. He believed without the young woman present, the old man was an easy target, so he made his move.

"What are those," Chris asked, stepped forward and grabbed the leather thong around Emrys' neck, pulling on the stones. They did not give way, so he pulled harder, and the old man fell forward into him.

"Let me see them!" Chris said, trying to get them over his head.

A hand released the cane, letting it fall to the floor, and he gently touched Chris's chest. Chris froze from head to toe like he was an ice sculpture. Emyrs whispered, "Release..." Chris opened his hand and Emyrs stood up fully, shook his head and steadied himself. He then raised his hand and said a word not in any vocabulary. As he said it, he looked into Chris's eyes and the memory of meeting the buyer came into focus in Emyrs mind as if he were Chris. He saw and heard the entire interaction. As he saw it Chris forgot it all. Then Chris also forgot the exchange with him and his student. He turned on his heels and, on the way out caught site of a small bag of cookies and helped himself to it. A gift for his troubles.

By the time Emyrs made it down the stairs his student had already began the hunt and he eaten the small bag of cookies. When she came downstairs, she reached into her bag and grabbed a small cannister. Spinning the top she rubbed a bit of the red powder on her fingers, pulled it out and threw it to the ground. She too used some words that could not be understood and as the red powder touched the concrete it made a flushing sound then it just moved. It made a path before her, and she followed it like a hound. She saw a small old tavern across the street and the powder led her there. It led her to the front door, but before she entered, she pulled out what looked like a pen, and drew a reverse question mark sigil upon the door jam that left no observable mark. When she entered the loud bar with about twenty people in it, she smelled it over all the smells of beer, filth, vomit, food, wine, spilled everything, it was magic.

Emyrs had stopped just outside the apartment, looking down he saw the red powder he had taught her to make and then he looked around and saw the scribe mark glowing at the door's entrance in the foreground. He walked hurriedly after it towards the bar.

It did not take her long to seek the origin of the smell, it led her to a barstool. Several men glared at her and she felt their heat. When she got to the bar, she smelled the magic again. A glass of scotch, neat, half drunk, his tip was still under the glass. She could smell him, kin? She thought he was kin? But how? The red glow went out the other door to the back of the bar, she was moving again towards it. As she pushed open the door Emrys called after her having just entered, but it was too late... "Morgan!"

As she stepped into the alley, she fell into the space in between. Before her in the mist was a middle-sized man in a Victorian style overcoat and top hat. He was facing her with his arms out in a cross pattern. An invitation to duel or die in the tradition of the Fey. He was kin. The shock made her hesitate, the drop into the space between, facing a fey, being challenged to a dual, and all without any notice. It was all so shocking.

She was caught unprepared, and he threw a dagger before she could even move or react. It slammed into her shoulder, throwing her off her feet, and nailed her to the door breaking her clavicle with a crack. It was of course, no ordinary blade. She was in a haze, she collapsed under it, only upright because she was pinned.

Removing the hat, he offered a large bow, his long hair falling from the hat. "At your service, Morgan. It has been some time since you pursued the likes of me," he stood up and for the first time she could see him. Ferrel.

"Do you know me lady?"

She could not answer, the poison, the magic, had subdued her, but she knew him. He was Ferrel, from the Court of the Queen. He was no prince, he was not even a lord, but he was in her court, and he was a slayer. She had gone too fast, unexpecting, thinking the magic she smelled was the jewel and not the person holding it. He would kill her, not like a human death, she could recover from that, he would remove and eat her soul. A slayer should not be toyed with. Suddenly she burst into tears, and this stopped Ferrel in his tracks. It was not out of pain, although she was enduring a ton of it. It was not out of fear. It was not even out of her regret. It was the pain of separation from her lord, and she knew she would pass on without the ability of learning from him and that was worse than death.

Ferrel considered this and his hesitation made him consider how he might enjoy the death more. He looked her over and took his time. The unbuttoning of the coat, he took hold of his time piece, not a clock, it was the thing that kept them in the place between. It was his shrewdest weapon. His tight face showing he was Fey, small, pointed ears, pointed jaw, unhuman features. She had them too but covered them with her makeup. He found this makeup and the covering of their kin to be disgusting.

Emrys had made his way to the door, struck it with the cudgel, pushed it in and saw the empty alley. He was not invited to the party apparently. He closed the door and struck it again. He did this over and over until he pushed it open and saw mist. Slamming the stick into the ground just as the bartender went to reach for him, he was in the breach, but he no longer held a cudgel, but a six-foot elder staff stopped with a ruby gem. As he entered Ferrel saw him and jumped back three feet.

"How dare you! You set a trap for someone half your age vermin! Offer me my property and I may allow you to leave!" Emrys stormed toward him, as the bartender looked into an empty alleyway.

At a distance Ferrel caught himself, grinning to his elder.

"You are not Fey, my lord, you have no power over..."

Before the small man could finish Emrys scowled his eyes and the red glow of the ruby engaged. The Fey recognized the gem and all at once fear rose into his face, and he raised his hands in a sign of giving up. It was too late; the spell was in play. Tethers rose from the ground and gripped the fey's limbs, opening him up and then it began to spread him until it became a bit painful when the fey screamed, "MERRRRRRR-LINNNNNN!!!!"

"Do not use my name Ferrell slayer!" the mage said, slamming the end of the staff on the earth, sparking the ground below.

"I am sorry my lord! I was only on a mission; it is not for me! I, I am just a flea in the court my lord, please!"

"You were going to kill her, Morgan Le Fey, you dog!" and with that he walked to Morgan and pulled the dagger out sharply and threw it into the earth grounding its power and allowing her to regain herself.

Morgan initially fell to the ground, released from the pin. It did not take long, Morgan's heart was much darker than Emyrs, and she would have her revenge. She reached out her hand and 6 feet away she enchanted his heart, felt the beat and began to squeeze until he screamed again.

"Morgan!" Emrys called, and she gripped a little more for effect and then released.

"Yes, my lord," she answered.

Emrys strode towards Ferrel, took hold of the fey's coat and opened it. He closed his eyes and called to his stone, and it began to glow in the inside pocket. The old man pulled it out and turned his back to the fey. He opened his own coat and reached inside his shirt to the waistband, pulling out an invisible object. He shook it and a six-inch silver handled knife was revealed. On its top were two more of the same rubies that mounted his staff as very small side stones but the third was supposed to be the missing garnet. It had been ripped off the top, and now returned. No ordinary gem, it was powered and forged with the blade in a very magical place. As it touched the silver it burned itself back into the hilt, he heard a new voice right after he looked up and saw the eyes widen and a deep intake of breath from Morgan...

"Well Merlin, you can't blame a woman for trying, can you?" her deep hard voice vibrated on the walls of the place in between. It was a place she ruled. She had the upper hand here. He was a lord, but she, is a Queen.

Without looking he turned and took a knee.

"My Lady," he said, head down.

"Your respect is very nice," she said, her wide dress dragging on the ground as she walked the area. She wore blue and black as her custom, wings on her back, she was full Fey. She was power. She walked by Ferrel, and he did not speak. Laying her hand on a tether, it released him dropping him to the ground. She waved a hand at Morgan and another crack put her collar bone back in place with a yipe from her, she too, took a knee. The Queen touched only Emrys. Her hand on his shoulder for a moment and then she was gone.

Ferrel took the moment to act, pulled at the clock and then only Emrys on a knee and Morgan on both knees were still in the back of the bar alley as the bartender threw the door open. For him no time had passed.

"You old bastard, those bangs on my door dinged the hell out of it! You're going to pay for that," he yelled and then noticed they were both on the ground. He looked puzzled. "I do apologize sir, I could not get out fast enough, not a very nice place you have there," Emrys said, crossed the distance and reached into the coat and handed the man a hundred-dollar bill, "I hope that will be enough sir."

The man looked at the money and at Emrys, unsure, he just turned and shut the door. Morgan rose and without a word they walked back to the subway and returned to their penthouse. They both fell into the bed exhausted.

"What is it with you and the Queen?" Morgan asked, not expecting much of a rely. His head lay on her stomach as she ran her fingers through his long gray and white hair. "It is a long story my love, for now, let's just say, my dagger was difficult to come by and she has always wanted it back."

CHAPTER THREE

"JACK GOES TO THE CORNER"

BY ROBERT HENRY

W E ALL REMEMBER THE story of Jack and the beanstalk: Where Jack, a young man living with his mother alone, trades their only cow in for a handful of magical beans. And the beans produce a beanstalk shooting into the clouds. To which, he climbs up into the clouds, stumbles upon a giant, a magic harp and a goose of golden eggs, climbs down, chops down the stalk killing the giant. And he and his mother live happily ever after. But is this the end of the story? Some sources suggest that it isn't. For immediately following Jack's triumph over the giant and acquisition of a golden egg laying goose, something unexpected happened.

For the very next night Jack lay in his bed ever so comfortable, thinking to himself how happy he was with how it turned out; stretching, yawning and then contently rolling over on his head. It was all like a distant dream with the silvery pale moonlight streaming in through a high window above. The quiet of night gave a low continuous hum as to pat ol' Jack on the head and kiss him good night. But just as he found himself falling away to sleep a gentle tapping echoed through the house. Jack froze as he heard footsteps accompany the series of knocks. "Creak!" went the front door as it was opened.

"Mother, she must've answered it." He thought to himself.

Jack heard two voices talking back and forth, but muddled. And he was half tempted to open his door and find out who it was and what they wanted. But only half tempted, the other more convincing half decided to sit there besides the conversation seemed, if agreeable, at least civil and thus non-threatening. And so paying little mind to the midnight disturbance, Jack wiggled back into position and fell fast asleep.

It wasn't until the next morning it was revealed. For as jack jumped out of bed, changed his clothes and stepped through the door of his room there was his mother waiting. She looked irritated and quite displeased.

"Jack!" She said.

He stood as a prisoner stands with uncomfortable guilt in front of a judge in court. She angrily tapped her foot and just stared at her son.

"Well, what do you have to say?"

Confused, Jack replied with a dopey, "What?"

"Don't give me that!" She barked back. "Do you know who came to the door last night?"

Jack shrugged his shoulders with a feigned indifference.

"A gentleman who lives up the road and although we'd never met, he was remarkably kind in spite of what you'd done."

Jack stiffened up as if he could get anymore confused.

"Done? What had I done?"

"As if you didn't know. The Goose! That precious goose that you stole from him!"

"What?!" Jack exclaimed. To which Jack then reminded his mother of that magnificent story of the beanstalk, the giant and how he'd *really* gotten the goose. She believed it then, for how could one hide the mile long fell stalk and veritably bottomless pit created by the giant. It had only been a day since the fall of the beanstalk and though she'd believed it then initially, given the evidence, this gentleman's story of the stolen goose seemed more sensible . And mothers always go with the more sensible as most likely.

Jack pleaded with his mother to believe him. For though what had happened was incredulous and extraordinary, Jack, above all, was thoroughly honest. And up until that point his behavior was unimpeachable, hi s mother rarely even raised her voice to the boy. So it came to a surprise to Jack for what followed.

In a burst of rage as punishment, a consequence Jack was hitherto completely foreign to, she said,

"Go to the Corner!"

The words echoed in Jack's head like church bells in a deep valley. The corner! How was he to go to the corner, he thought. There wasn't any room. The area where two walls meet left no space at all. Nevertheless, being an obedient lad, with head bowed in shame, he slowly walked towards the corner.

The first thing he noticed was he couldn't merely 'walk' there. For the two conjoining walls bumped the right and left of his head to where he could step no further. And had Jack been unconcerned with obeying his mother, he would have stopped right there. But no, he was determined to go 'into' it. So he pushed and pushed and pushed; not on either wall but in the space where they met. Jack's face pressed against the two walls and left him blind until right before him the dark space grew into a starry night and outside air. Harder and harder he leaned into it until, huddled as closed as he could get, the inward walls spread outward, as if into or out of nowhere-which one he couldn't tell. The walls vanished revealing an open field extending for miles, couched between two forests-or the field breaking the forest like a stream through the dry. Jack had gone into the corner.

It was remarkably large and in view of his being in the corner he thought nothing of it to explore the field and forest of his punishment. And so he ran through the grassy expanse all the while staring up at the overarching sky of stars. And upon a closer glance he noticed some of the larger stars had faces, animated and with personalities of their own. He further noticed they seemed to be talking to one another; and listening as well as he could he caught a faint whisper here and there. But unfortunately Jack was so caught up with the stars and their magnificent display of human like qualities, he failed to watch where he was walking-if walking is the right word for though his pace lessened it was still a healthy gallop. And in consequence the preoccupied youth left the field and into the forest. Well it was long before he came in contact with one of its inhabitants.

"Bam!" The boy ran smack dab into a towering elm tree, throwing him to the ground. Dazed, Jack shook his head and tried to get up but found something holding him back; it was the tree branch. It had grabbed hold of him, wrapping its knotted arm around his with snaps and pops. It swung him in the air and sat him on his feet, as it held him there. He tried to break free but to no avail. But something else happened. He then heard a voice.

"They only do that 'cuz they want somethin'"

Jack turned around, for by then the elm had released the hold on him in response to the voice, and standing behind him, only coming up to about his knee, was a plate! It had two arms, two legs and the rest was a face. As if a walking talking plate was natural, he addressed it.

"What does he want?" Pointing back at the tree which had accosted him.

"He wants you to go fetch him a pail of water I suspect. It is dry at this time of night and he is probably very thirsty."

"O I see." He said.

"Where are you going by the way?" Which Jack thought it strange of the plate to ask without first asking his name. He said, "Nowhere particular, just exploring."

"Oh." The plate said, almost as if disappointed with his response, throwing a subtle frown. "Well in all your 'exploring' have you seen a spoon?"

"A Spoon?" Jack asked confusedly.

"Yes, I seem to have lost him and need to make it back."

"Back where?"

"Back..." He stopped short of replying. "Forget it. Could you help find him?" As if too hurried to explain.

"Sure but I don't know where to look."

"No matter, you're much taller than I so I figured you'd spot him before me."

Jack rubbed his chin and shook his head in agreement. "True."

"This way. I think he went in this direction." And Jack followed the shiny little plate glowing like a concave moon captured and shrunk by the jealous earth. With bowed legs it wobbled ahead of him.

"So how did you lose him?" Jack asked as they moved through the field.

Preoccupied however the plate hurriedly answered with, "The Wind."

"The wind?"

The plate stopped and turned towards Jack aggravated but determined to put to rest his cumbersome questions.

"We were in the meadow and the wind scattered us abroad. I went this way and he..."

The dish pointed in the direction they were heading, turned away from Jack and continued walking. Jack, somewhat satisfied with his answer, shrugged his shoulders and followed. The grass was thick and tall, waving in the winds of the corner that swept across the meadow. The dish, unintentionally acting like a sail, caught the wind and was flung up, up in the air like a Frisbee. But Jack seized the porcelain disc in mid flight and set him back on the ground. So, this time the dish walked sideways with his narrow thin side to the wind. His eyes watering up as the gusts of wind irritated his eyes like a ripe exposed onion. But the dish, like a disciplined soldier, marched on through the thicket.

Just then, in the distance, Jack spotted a shiny object in between the sways of grass like hair in the wind.

"I think I see something."

The dish strained his eyes but couldn't see.

"What is it?" He asked with animated earnest.

"I don't know, lets get closer."

Jack led the way to the shiny object with the dish carefully creeping behind. The closer they got, the clearer they could see what it was. It was a spoon! It, like the dish, had two sets of appendages, but with its face set deep in the concave of the implement. The dish rushed up to the spoon, but as soon as the two touched both sets of appendages retracted into their bodies and the faces disappeared. And since either had legs or arms anymore, they fell flat; the dish on the cushioned grass and the spoon on top of him.

Jack rushed over to the two and tried his best to revive the dish but it was no use. For whatever life was in the china, it was gone. He suspected it had something to do with the two, the dish and the spoon, being reunited and I would have to agree with him. So Jack snatched up the two, tucked them under his arm and marched off into the meadow. For he remembered what the dish had said of where he was before being separated from the spoon. And so he thought it right to do his best to take them back there; as that Jack always did his best to do the right thing. Though where it was, he had no idea. But he was confident that he would find it. After all, aren't all dishes and spoons stored in drawers, cupboards, and kitchen counters? So surely such places would be easy to spot in a meadow.

He hadn't gotten far before Jack spotted something like a fence running in a blocked formation in the meadow. It was some distance away, and the closer he got the more he recognized it as a pen of sorts. Inside the pen were about a dozen sheep or so. But unlike ordinary livestock, these were sitting in chairs seated around several sets of tables topped with dainty tasteful tablecloths. The sheep were working their hooves more like hands than feet, holding cups and saucers like gentlemen lounging with tea and conversation.

Jack resituated the dish and spoon as that they began slipping from underneath his arm and he unlatched a lock where a gate cut into the wall of the pen swinging open. The sheep paid little attention to him as he entered the pen, busily attending to their business and their numerous conversations. He overheard one or two of the conversations, accidentally of course for Jack was no eavesdropper usually. One table of sheep was discussing a recent rainstorm which evidently flooded one pasture where the sheep were accustomed to traveling through. Another table, in contrast, entertained the subject of a pair of unfaithful sheep, the content of which Jack found far to vulgar to pay attention to and so ignored it.

But off to himself, Jack saw a lone sheep sitting in a chair facing the opposite direction of the others weeping. The poor creature was hunched over with its hooves cupping his face and snout. And so Jack, compelled by something like duty but more like pity, walked over to console it.

"What's wrong?"

The sheep's face rose out of from his hands or hooves, which were filled with sheepish tears.

"They're gone."

"What's gone?" He asked.

"My dish and spoon. I can't eat...everyone else has and I can't...I just can't..." He started to tear up again. And from what I understand sheep are probably the most emotional of all farm animals. "I'm so hungry." He continued with sniffles and coughs. "A dish and a spoon you say." The sheep humbly nodded.

"Well it wouldn't happen to be this dish and spoon?" And Jack pulled out the two from underneath his arms.

The sheep brightened up considerably and smiled a full crescent and a half of a smile. He took the pair, giving Jack yet another smile of gratitude and asked if he would excuse him. To which the sheep got up from his chair and walked over to another table. Jack hadn't noticed it before, but it was a long table with all sorts of food items laid out such as one would see at a buffet. The sheep looked over each, scratched his chin with each selection, would pick up the implement on each dish, scoop up a portion and slide it on his plate. Once the plate was filled, though not too full, for he was a well mannered sheep, he returned to his chair, nodded to Jack who looked off in the distance as the wooly creature delicately and carefully ate his meal.

Once finished, the sheep carefully walked the plate over to a pile, where many others lay, sat it down, produced a handkerchief from the fluff where a pocket would be, dabbed his lips with it and walked back to jack.

"O I can't thank you enough. I hadn't eaten a thing all day."

Jack thought to himself how queer it was a sheep was eating people food and not grass. But he wasn't interested in asking the sheep since he thought it may be rude. And besides more than likely he wouldn't know anyways. For who knows why it is one prefers steak over chicken or beans over broccoli. It is a matter of taste and there is no accounting for it.

The two sat and talked for a while, but not about anything important. It was chiefly the sheep who was listing all of his various aches and pains that he suffered as a result of what he called grazing; which to him was nothing more than standing in a field-though to a person it would mean he was eating the grass. Jack didn't really think the sheep knew what the word meant but again he didn't wish to correct him.

But right after he finished his thought Jack spotted something like a rope drop down from the sky right behind the sheep. Jack looked to see where it ended, but it went on as far as he could see; though it was night and thus hard to see. The sheep noticed Jack looking behind and turned to see what it was. And indifferently turned back towards Jack.

"O that's just from the moon. The man who lives up there uses it to shimmy down every once in a while, then he climbs back up once he's done doing whatever it is he does."

"The man on the moon?" Jack inquired.

"Yes. I am sure you've seen him. Poor thing, stuck up there all the time. Must be frightfully boring. I guess that's why he comes down here. A lot more space down here I suppose."

As the sheep went on about the man and how he mysteriously, and sometimes annoyingly, traveled from moon to ground, Jack's interest was piqued. He again looked up the rope, it dangling in the dark sky like a limp branch swaying in the wind. And while it looked like a long, long way up, he had seen the man on the moon. Though it was far away he had looked old. And if he could make the climb, surely Jack could. So, he explained to the sheep what he was intent on doing; which resulted in a simple nod and subtle affirmation.

"Ok. But if you do, please tell him not use that cart again."

"He uses a cart?" Jack asked.

"Yes. On occasion. One time in particular he used it to tote some livestock...or at least a cow...one I know of. It nearly fell on me. Very dangerous thing it is."

Jack thought little of this, but still there was a suspicion, in the back, far back, of his thinker which got him thinking. But the thoughts were so faint, like a ship from a foggy distance, that he paid little mind to it at the moment. And yet, if he only knew what it would mean to him once he made it to the top where the moon hung. It would soon all make sense.

But presently Jack was in the mood for adventure and to surprise the man on the moon, or at least see him if even he didn't see him. And so Jack took a hold of the rope, gripping it with a strong hand and pulled himself up. One hand over another, Jack made the climb. But he found the way far easier than he had thought it would be. For he had countless times pulled himself up ropes hanging out of trees or off the side of ledges and this was far less difficult than those had been. And he was quite relieved since it turned out to be a long way up to the top. Fortunately it was dark out, otherwise the height from which he dangled would have utterly scared him silly. Yet, he continued the climb like a skilled acrobat. Up, up he went, just like the time he scaled the beanstalk. But this time it was far less stable.

One hand, two hands, three, over another and then he came to the surface of the moon. It was much smaller than he thought. In fact it was about the size as it looked from below, but as he got to the walking it seemed to widen as the light from a lantern does when one turns a corner. And the global field he walked on, which glowed with the florescence of night but was immediately swallowed by the dark, came to an abrupt end. For in front of him stood a towering wall with a series of windows, like those of an ancient castle, but instead of rock it was made out of the strange moon material.

Out of one of the windows, Jack heard a voice. He quietly crept up to it as to listen. And as was mentioned earlier, he was not by nature an eavesdropper, but in the situation he felt compelled, by some strange force, to listen and not be heard. So, he leaned up to the edge of the sill and listened. The voice was that of a man, talking to himself about something he'd done. He said,

"Well, I wonder if I'll have to go back down there again. After all, she seemed convinced that he'd stolen it." He laughed to himself. "Yes, because in a way he had, just not from me. It was from Ol' Brown. I mean when I sold that boy Jack those beans, I had no idea *that* would happen. I figured Ol' Brown would capture the lad, like we had agreed, eat him and I would get my fill of the gold he promised. But no, he had to chop down the stalk and kill him. By godfrey, I would just go over there and take it now, but Ol' Brown's brother Brown Tom moved in and he doesn't know me. O well, it doesn't matter now, I'll have that goose the next time I go down and that boy's great feat will have been in vain."

With that he laughed again.

Jack did everything in his power to stay quiet. He wanted nothing more than to run in there and attack the man. For it was him after all, all him. He had planned it all. He sold him the magic beans. It was he who had conspired with the giant to bring an Englishman up to his cloud lair and become a meal for that vicious giant. And it was he who had lied to his mother about the goose.

And as Jack was thinking what to do, he heard a "moo!" and a kick. "Shut up you stupid cow. Once I get all the milk I can out of you, I'll cut ya' up and make steaks from you."

Jack then knew where he had gotten the cow. It was the very same one he had sold him for the beans. For just as the sheep had explained, the livestock was lifted up; his livestock.

Jack immediately began hatching a plan to retrieve the cow. But just as he was sorting out the details he heard footsteps approaching behind him. As he turned, it was too late, the man on the moon was right there, in front of him.

"Jack, my boy." He said with the deepest sarcasm. "How did you find me up here?"

"It was a punishment." Jack replied with a short, but truthful

answer.

"O I see." He replied as he circled the boy looking him up and down. "Well its a shame you can't leave. There is no way down back down the way you came...or at least I won't let you leave."

As he made this last remark, he produced a dagger from the back of his britches and pointed it at the boy.

"Now look here....you aren't going anywhere...for you see I have much work to do up here...there are fields to dust, stars to polish, the sun needs to be lit every morning...and I am tired of doing it myself...if you refuse..." He tightened his grip on the knife and thrust it in his direction as to threaten. "...i'll take it out on your mother. She has taken a liking to me. And I would hate to hurt her...but...if you don't cooperate...well..."

But just as he was talking, fortune struck ol' Jack, and misfortune the man on the moon. For the man was perspiring so much he created a puddle of sweat that settled right in front of his feet. And as he walked towards the boy, he slipped in the puddle, fell down and back on his head, to where, he was knocked out cold. So, one could say that his own desperation produced perspiration, which led to his expiration.

As the man lay on the ground, Jack knew he hadn't much time. So he ran into the man's house, frantically looked for the cart which he had used to tote the cow up to the moon, wheeled it out, went back in and pulled the cow out by its muzzle, and proceeded to goad the cow atop the cart. Once atop it, Jack carefully attached the rope to a pulley which the man on the moon presumably used to hoist goods up and down from the moon, and slowly eased the cow down from the moon.

The cow swayed back in forth, between stars and astral lights of every hue shooting through the night sky. The low pitched creak of each pendulum like revolution struck a nerve in the boy, afraid to death the man on the moon would catch him. But it wasn't long before the cow safely made it to the soft grass of the meadow. And while I am sure many scientists and 'sensible' people will criticize the feat, for afterall the moon is so far away from the earth or so they say, little do they know what every child knows about the moon. For to look up at that celestial disc with an everlasting glow and unending supply of bliss, one immediately gathers the impression that to visit it would be more like a dream-like ascension into the heavens, than to be propelled up to it with rockets and forceful forces. The universe, like a gentleman, acts in accord to how its treated. And I imagine that Mr. Armstrong hardly saw the moon as it 'really' is anymore than a frightened child expresses his true feelings to a bully who aggressively demands his lunch money.

Anyway, the cow made it safely to the ground, letting out a gentle moo, only mildly upsetting the sheep who were still sitting in leisure at their respective tables. And now it was Jack's turn. He spit in his right hand and rubbed in his left as he grabbed for the rope. But, just then, the man on the moon came to and groggily stumbled to his feet. Once he looked over at the rope and Jack climbing down grabbed for his arms, as to pull him up.

"O no you don't my boy!" He caught hold of his hand. "I got ya', you little rascal." But as he was pulling him towards him, a shooting star with a thrust like an arrow of Diana, or like the providence of God, brushed up against the side of the man's leg, burning him and causing him to trip and fall. And as he did, he let go the hold he had on Jack. Well, Jack saw his chance and got back on the rope and slid down like a fireman's pole. And while it proved effective, as that, he landed safely in the meadow in a matter of seconds, the boy received a smart pair of rope burns on his hands.

He ran around the meadow in circles screaming in pain when one of the sheep, the one he'd returned the dish and the spoon to, rushed towards him with a pitcher of water.

"Here, this will help." And dousing the scorched palms with midnight's coolest water, a sigh of relief came across the boy. He sat down at one of the tables with the sheep, who began to feed him and feed him, remarking at how wonderful a feat it truly was of his shooting down the rope like that.

"And look." One of the sheep pointing the rope coiled up and in pieces lying in the field. "The rope got so hot it tore into. Its a shame. I guess the old man on the moon will never come back down here again."

But to Jack it was no shame at all. In fact, he was quite happy. For certainly he could keep the goose and he had gotten the cow back. Indeed he had gotten more than the night after the beanstalk fell.

After eating and talking with the sheep, Jack knew he had to return home. He thanked the sheep for their hospitality, and being that sheep are incredibly polite as they are sensitive, they to showered him with politeness and farewells. And so, Jack went through the meadow, back to where he had come into the corner, which returning was much easier since by pushing his way into the corner, all he had to do was go to the very spot and pull.

He immediately appeared in the area between two walls with himself and the cow. But fortunately his mother was in the other room, otherwise she would have got the fright of her life at seeing a cow come through a corner. And so he called to his mother and she came in to the room. Seeing the cow, she was equally surprised and happy. And Jack's story was more readily received with cow in hand.

Years later, as Jack grew up, wealthy of course, he would often look up at the moon, and see the old man that had tricked him so many years ago. But now he is trapped never to trick the world of man again. Perhaps he has learned his lesson. For if he has I suspect he would be a pleasant man to know, for he still works hard at grooming the stars, relighting the sun everyday and singing little children to sleep with his songs of nighttime that are only audible to children...everywhere.

The end

CHAPTER FOUR

"BLOOD AND FIRE"

BY KERRY PURDY

THE YOUNG MAN WHO had been caught in a crossfire as he attempted to throw water on flames was bleeding out, and I thought I could save him. That was, until the bucket fell over. The bucket filled with water that was mostly bloody... I thought I could hold myself together just a bit longer. But the fumes were getting to me. Not just the smoke billowing through the city...but the stench of the blood.

In my haze, I don't know what happened. Was it me in my delirium from the heat, the exhaustion, the hunger brought on by the sight and scent of the blood? Was it another one of the civilian volunteers who had stayed behind in the city to fight the flames and drag the injured to safety? Whoever had knocked over the bucket of water that I had been using to clean the wounds of the wounded firefighter? The water that was now mostly...blood? I looked at the reddish pool longingly. I was about to dip a finger in it and lick it until...

"Noo Callie, stay with us, *a cailin!*" I thought I heard the voice of my brother, felt him grasping my shoulder and shaking me. He was the only other one present that knew...but then again, he didn't. He hadn't inherited the bloodlust that I had. He didn't have to daily drink water from the special goblet that my grandparents had brought to the Colonies...the only thing that could quench my family's bloodlust...and now that the British had attacked and burned the city, who knew if it had survived.

"Callie! He's too far gone!" I felt my brother drag me to my feet and pull me away. I wanted to bite him...bite him and drink his blood, the sweet nectar of life. I at least needed to get away from the commotion to do what I had to do, and Patrick knew that. But then again, in all this commotion, who would notice a young woman drinking blood?

When we were just a few yards away from the wounded man that I had been attempting to treat, who alas, as Patrick said, was too far gone, I grabbed my knife out of my dress pocket and lunged at Patrick. My dear wee brother yelped, but stood fast. I jammed the blade into his shoulder and as the bright, warm liquid ran out, I ran my hand into it. I licked my brother's blood off of my hand greedily. He rolled his eyes as I drank my fill, but he understood.

All was back to normal. My bloodlust had been quenched...for now. The goblet couldn't be burning along with the rest of Washington, D.C., could it? No...the hand of Dian Cecht himself forged it. It could survive.

Patrick chuckled ruefully at me as we began making our way back through the hell-scape.

"The things that I do for ya, *cailin.*"

"I couldn't do it without ya, *A Chuisle,*" I responded. There were plenty of more injured to tend, not to mention fires to put out and the lone British to hold off. Speaking of which...were those flames leaping up from President Madison's house?

CHAPTER FIVE

"TWO COILS, TWISTED"

BY MIR PLEMMONS

ANNIE SAT IN HER old, overstuffed chair – tiny, tucked up and nestled in it, as always. The lamp table was in easy reach, with her battered record player and her beloved 33s. Today was a day for Billie Holiday – Annie was feeling every single one of her 82 years, and full of memories. Gold joys, red passions and pains, brown endurances. She was in her autumn time of life. She'd decided that when she turned 75.

As "It's Easy to Remember" wound down, her eyes turned toward the next record. She was going to play "Fine and Mellow", but the air today had a tense stillness. It reminded her of something, but the something wouldn't come clear. She was tired. She turned the record over and put it on to play but then dozed off. She dreamed all reds and browns: Billie sang of strange and bitter fruit on the poplar tree that Annie, as a lady, did not like to recollect. She awoke, disoriented, to a rising storm to the North.

***

CLEM WAS OUT FISHING. Well, now, when you're livin' slow on the lake, and the next load of pots ain't owed to the shop for another week – any still morning can keep you later on the water than you meant. No harm done, is there? Still... he looked above the trees on the South side of the lake, at those clouds building up trouble. Best get back to the house. This Spring – if it was Spring – kept bringing the darnedest weather. He didn't plan to get caught out.

He unshipped the oars, and began the even, steady pulls of long practice. Rowing is meditative, and the weather reminded him of Sarah. She'd played with words, the only one but his mother who called him Clement. She said it, laughing, and laughed more when she called him Inclement. He shook his head to clear it, and rowed harder.

He beached the boat, hauled it up and lashed it down. He wondered when he'd be able to just snub its line to the dock cleat and be done. Not any time soon, he figured. He stopped by the shed on his way up to the house. He usually did, after Sarah came back to mind. He'd built the pottery studio – wheel, shelves, everything there but the new kiln – years ago. Built for her. His favorite photo of her, a little faded now, sat on the sill. He touched it and wondered again if he threw pots because he liked the feel of the clay all that much, or because when he touched it he touched her.

***

ANNIE FOUND HERSELF URGENTLY collecting her coat and hat, listening to the rising wind. She didn't know what was driving her outside; she was sure as sure the siren would start any minute, and she really was getting too old for this. It might be early in the year, but this storm had ...intentions. Regrettably, it didn't matter. She didn't ignore those hunches, not anymore. Whatever the price for answering the call, the price for ignoring wasn't one she was willing to pay. She shoved into her good sturdy shoes, dismissed the umbrella, then trotted downstairs and out the door.

Her feet took her the few blocks to the town's heart, through gritty winds that were, as yet, unfocused and deniable. Annie and the old bandstand had sidestepped a score of storms together. She dropped onto a bench to catch her breath. Too old for this. The autumn time of one's life is not for running, being out in storms or dam'fool idealistic crusades. On cue, the tornado siren came to life 60 yards away, on the ex-firehouse. Beneath the thunderheads to the Northeast, a downward roiling point gathered, and the sky took on a greenish cast.

***

C LEM'S HEAD SNAPPED UP. Outside the South-facing window, the sky had gone green. He berated himself. Here he'd been, woolgathering in the pottery shed, while the wind's fingers explored its eaves with increasing interest. It took the siren's distant wail to shake him loose and force him to pay attention.

He wrenched the door open against the wind's pull and paused, staring at the storm. The winds were getting high and hungry though he couldn't make out a funnel cloud. Some reluctance held him back from the cellar, but he sure couldn't stay in this shed. As if to make that point, the wind gave the shed a good, hard yank, getting serious about it. He looked up in time to see a tornado descend, looking like nothing so much as a horse's pizzle. Past time to get out of this shed and to real cover He had to make it to the storm cellar, and he knew he couldn't afford the time he'd lost. With a grimace, he reached back, grabbed the photo and stuffed it in his coat pocket. Jamming his cap down low, Clem braced himself and stepped into the full force of the storm.

***

THE BANDSTAND STOOD IMPERVIOUS, above this swirling of wind and leaf, paper and branch – and seemingly limitless dirt. Trashcans rolled and clanged, and a window screen cartwheeled crazily down the street. Annie kept her head down. Her work didn't require seeing the winds, not exactly. She settled back into herself, reaching deep down. She'd done this for decades, after all. It had its own ways and rhythms.

Her grandmother's proud, weathered face – older even than Annie was now – shone in her mind, joined by a chanting voice that rolled Hausa words to meet American realities. Her grandmother always said the rain on a tin roof reminded her of the music of her childhood, two lifetimes and two continents ago. Grandmother's pride was more than equal to the task of holding onto language and skills through dangerous decades of hiding both but using both to protect her town, and gladly bringing it forth when time ripened, to teach the child who listened.

Now the words came, words of stability and safety, of community and protection. She built walls for her town with words and rhythms that grew out of ways to keep prowling beasts away at night. Grandmother was a blessing to the whole town, though they'd never known the half of it. She'd say that's as it should be. The storm faded from Annie's awareness, partly as she got to work, and partly in response to it. The winds' skirts twirled away from Annie and the bandstand, losing the pace of their dance. Annie kept pushing, chanting, rolling the words against the thundering voice of the twister as it tried to set its plough against the Northern edge of town. Annie knew her craft, and smoothly spread Grandmother's power to protect her home again. She'd see to it. The tornado would miss.

***

ON THE OTHER SIDE of the storm, Clem's slog against the wind suddenly shifted. He was knocked sideways, and tumbled like a kicked dog into a ditch his tractor'd left in all the doggone rain. Hurting, he gathered himself and started to crawl toward the cellar. The storm had jumped toward him and started grinding its way over his fields. He was going to have to be smart; this was big trouble and little time. As he moved, he noticed the wind had ripped his coat when it threw him. He checked, in a moment of realization: the photograph was gone from his pocket. Normally a mild, sad man, the sound that burst forth was a decades-old dam breaking. The "NO!" that ripped loose from him shook the very sky.

A sudden stillness wrapped Clem, the shed (minus a section of roof) and a circle a good seventy feet in all directions. He still could hardly see the house, but he sure could see the grass pulled and stripped around him. Nothing moved in his circle. Clem's overworked brain stuttered to a stop. His circle?! His circle!? ...What? Dazed, he groaned his way up and staggered to where the startled wind had dropped his picture. Maybe it was Sarah's circle, instead. He half-collapsed half-sank to the ground, gathered in the picture and curled around it, holding it in his lap.

Touching it brought him back to a shred of pragmatism, anyway. He had to get to shelter before whatever-it-was that made this circle just wasn't, anymore. The cellar was still outside his doubtful safe zone, though as he looked he realized the winds were no longer going in the same direction. The storm seemed to be splitting around him. He looked up. And up. And up. A narrow glimpse of clear sky could be seen, way up there. He tried to gather himself. He really ought to do something, not just sit there on the wet grass with a broken picture frame in a cone of silence. He just couldn't figure what.

***

HER FOCUS FRAYED WHEN the storm did. Something was very different, this time. The storm stopped moving away, rebounded, and then – there was a sudden eddy of stray winds off the cloud's North side. Within a minute, a small funnel started coming down to gather them. Now she had two cyclones to manage, and they were fighting her. Worse, she was tired and the tornado was pushing, trying to backtrack on her. This was new. New wasn't good. Not when only an old woman stood between the town and two funnels.

Annie mentally shook herself by the scruff of the neck. She'd built her life on being determined. She wasn't having any of this nonsense! Resolve firmed, she pushed back. This time, the storm could not smoothly slip away from a small zone and leave her town safe. She'd have to do more, and quickly, while she still had a bit of energy. Then she'd rest. She would have to. Her energy was dipping dangerously low.

***

CLEM WAS STILL SITTING in his yard. He didn't seem to be able to make himself get up. It wasn't pain – he'd ache later from the wind throwing him, but not yet. What was this? Why was he so exhausted? That question seemed a lot safer than any questions about the still circle around him. Thinking of it, he looked out. The winds were still whipping field and lawn past the circle, but he was now between the first tornado and a new mini-tornado. He hadn't even noticed.

He slowly realized he was feeling more pressured, stressed, like there was something he needed to do or he'd be back in danger. Everything still seemed too abstract, and he thought he might be in shock, but something was niggling at him. He tried to force himself to look more closely. It took a minute for him to find it: the circle was shifting. The big tornado was coming toward him, and pushing on the circle. He wondered if it would collapse. Not a good thought. If it was somehow his circle, could he help it? Clem looked at the edge of the circle. Experimentally, he imagined it as a pot on the wheel, and his hand, smoothed with slip, easing its wall gently outward. That felt right. It might be easier if he just lay down, so he tried that. He mentally set his shoulders and feet as if all of him was his hand, and shoved. The circle moved back. Encouraged, Clem shoved harder. Maybe he could move it far enough to get to the cellar! He crawled out of the ditch, stood gingerly, and walked toward it, still pushing. Step by step, the circle moved, and step by step he got closer to safety. Just to be careful, he pushed the circle a yard past the cellar door before splitting his attention to lift it. Climbing down while focusing on the circle felt like a huge risk, but with no choice in the matter, he managed. Once inside and latched down, he collapsed into the chair and stopped pushing. Immediately, the storm was overhead, a freight train coming out of a tunnel. Clem was just glad that he was finally safe inside his!

***

A NNIE ROCKED FORWARD SUDDENLY, gave a last burst of energy and fell off the bench. She'd lost control of the storm, and her shield collapsed. She had nothing left to give, no energy and no ideas. All she could do was lay there and breathe, and even that seemed difficult. It was the bandstand's turn to protect her, she thought, as she drifted down.

Strong winds knocked through the town, bringing hail with them and flinging frozen softballs nearly sideways as it chased the tornado. Cars and houses were damaged, as was the bandstand. As it passed, the only person caught outside was Annie. She found herself lying on the floor, accompanied by hailstones. She felt cool, but it was nice, sort of restful. She needed rest. The white and grey of the bandstand and the hailstone by her head was soothing, wintery. She wondered dully about the red splash. Red belonged in fall, and Annie felt that she'd been too long in fall. It was time for winter. It was time for rest. She'd rest, now. Rest. That was a good thought. She decided she wouldn't get up for a bit, she'd just settle down for a good winter's sleep.

***

THE NEXT DAY, CLEM assessed damage and started picking up. He'd been so tired he fell asleep in the cellar and had to fumble for the flashlight to get breakfast and let himself out in the morning. He had no idea how long he'd slept. The pottery shed had lost its roof and a window, but was surprisingly intact. Even a good third of his pots had survived! His house was missed – just a gutter torn loose. A few unknown scrapes along his truck. He was pretty lucky – there for a while, he'd thought he was in serious trouble. He set Sarah's picture back in its place in the shed and started sweeping.

He even got his newspaper, if a few hours late. The headline was, of course, the tornados and the final hail. Clem read that the North side of near every building in town was damaged. There was also a death notice. Seems an old lady got caught out in the storm, knocked in the head by a 3▯ hailstone while trying to shelter in that old, broken down bandstand. That was a pity. Poor old lady. Clem folded up the paper and got back to work.

The vision for the short was two lives that never realized they were impacting each other — one protagonist was trained and experienced but tired; and the other had just the instinctive reaction of a crisis awakening.

Concept: There's a page from the town newspaper as a postlude, with her obit and a coil pot he donated to city hall with the two funnels leaning against each other and a pile of hailstones against the side opposite the small funnel.

CHAPTER SIX

"MEETING THE GRAND REDACTOR"

BY BENJAMIN NORMAN PIERCE

KLUFFT SAT IN THE little greypink metal chair outside the very important door, kneading his hands as though some finer process might be worked out there, best lubricated with primordial sweat (*but not so primordial, Klufft? You've had all scent tweaked away too...*)

Another set of hands, beyond that door, held the fate of Species X-33990-YYT-3909—the ones he hoped to see named "the Wise and Benign Polyps"--if Gates, the Grand Redactor would approve their resurrection from what the fossils and samples had offered up—if he would allow this so-nearly-sentient species to be uplifted, made not just a Herd or Crop or—Serendipity Forbid—a Sample or even Productors or Drones--but a Folk—despite the fact that Species X-33990-YYT-3811-a—the Malign Ovipositors Klufft had labeled them—had managed full sentience and had destroyed Hsu's World before the WBP's could ever have their own chance--

Klufft wanted a sense of justice—a sense he had made a difference—either one, he acknowledged, no longer sure in any part of his skin that these could be the same—he just wanted to make one genome he advocated for something more than a utility or a novelty—had he overstepped himself in seeking to make the Benign Polyps a Folk?—when they might not be resurrected—but be given "the Chuck"--genetic traces washed away or holyarked back at Sol station--

The Chuck—what advocate could refer to it without feeling sick—and it was the man on the other side of the door, Great Redactor Gates himself—who had spoke it so often and so clipped and crassly that he, he had breathed that term into common use.

It used to be called "The Charlie" or "do the Charles"--after Charles Darwin, of course...*which, now that I think of it makes no sense anyway* though Klufft. *It's human selection, not natural selection at all...*Now it just meant a tossing away, with Darwin's ghost grimacing in the background--

--rumor was that the Redactor was *Charles* Gates coming up in the world---

Some thought the new term made it more—human? More thinkable anyway—turning a formality into a buddyish nickname—Klufft was sure he knew better because he knew Gates, he felt, in his gut, had tried to feel even for him—The Chuck was the only word clipped enough or short enough—dismissive enough-- to suit him.

Everyone knew that Gates had run more nanos on his genome than anyone else would be allowed to—no-one was sure quite what he had done. Klufft felt sure that only he felt how much humanity Gates had edited out—maybe he had added nothing in fact, but had only amputated--

Klufft was partly immune from having his own tweaks inspected—none of it had yet been mandated, even psychopaths and addicts having slots to suit them waiting—Klufft could have tamped down considerable anxiety, for example, as he knew so sharply, so wetly just now--

--but I know what I must say, in what order—and don't call him Grand. That offends his contrived modesty, his pretense of service--

But anxiety is my conscience—isn't it? What would my Wise and Benign Polyps have used for morality, I wonder--

If they were made a Folk, though, some of that would be designed for them, before they had signs of volition emerge—was that right—did he have the right to make them moral so they could *be--*

But such was the prerogative of the system, and of the Grand Redactor beyond the door.

It had always been understood that ethics, morality—it was how the mind shaped the total being in the presence of a temptation—but when you could rewrite the biological place the temptations came from--

Bred first, morality later when the Academy joke—well leaked out to the labor classes by now...

From one point of view, though, "nature", such as it was, had "chosen" to lick the planet clean of most life except for some tight places in stone, some hang-outs far under the now-airless and lifeless waves, some lobes of lava yet lived---

But my client, they did not have the chance to participate in their own destruction---or their own resurrection, said a voice he tamped down--

Despite the expectations of every bit of classicist science fiction that had kept Klufft sane, when humanity got the stardrive just in time to infect the rest of the galaxy, it seemed all sentience everywhere had been just as insane or stupid or starved for oblivion. Every planet that had ever developed industry was ruined or it's way to ruin, and only homo sapiens, for no sapient reason, had alone had the luck to find both the stardrive and the key to nanogenetics—only a fanatic few could look back and feel any sense of destiny in it—everyone sweated out the feeling no more luck would be so dumb.

Every other intelligent species ever met had tweaked themselves to live in whatever deadly broth-and-desert they had turned their own world into, or they lived as eternal exiles in the few starships they had thrown out if they had found the warp rather than the tweak.

--and so now humanity chose which genomes to resurrect.

The very important door flickered and went translucent.

The hour had come and Kluffts' mouth tasted like the ruined world he had warped from just this Standard.

The Grand Redactor had thin, thin lips, pale like wax, sealed, like the word of God that issued from them, eyes that washed away whatever color they had by the glare—bags under the eyes that had plainly been kept for youth had been stitched in everywhere else—hair as golden as they day the Redactor had obtained adulthood—the rest massaged, fixed, archetypal, but in no way of note--

Klufft did not look like so much himself, he knew.

Klufft somehow sat down, he must have done, there he was--

"You are here to advocate—not only general resurrection for a species—but uplift to a Folk." he said, staring through Klufft, giving no invite even as the force-bench before his desk flickered into reality. Somehow, the Grand Redactor had cut through—not protocol, not formality, those, yes, too—but Klufft's planned order, his plan of presentation—just the facts then, the core, the essence—what this was about anyhow--

"I feel they have merit, Redactor" somehow he had just saved his own career, omitting the 'grand'--now to save the Polyups, wise, benign—they would be, they would--"I know them to be unique—ahm, in how they apprehended the outside world—and they were—ahm, biologically resourceful, adaptable, hearty, hale--" Then, if silence could stammer, it did so in his mouth.

The Redactor made some kind of no-change in his face that indicated a flicker of interest.

"Biological adaptivity is good in drones, as far as that goes—uplift to Folk, as you rightly apprehend, is first based on a contribution to be made by their subjectivity—the whole of life must be fixed, these days—and the load is too much—how would their unique point of view aid us in what we must do?"

Their point of view—the bouquet of their innermost—was that a stirring of humane insight inj the Redactor?--no--that was too much hope—the client must be saved—and here he was at the core he had to defend, on it's own merits—wasn't that enough?

"They could sense gravity—I don't want to guess which of our senses it would approximate—maybe some of the mo-tor/somatic subjectivities we know—but I am fairly sure it was co-efficient with their capacity for pattern-tracking and abstractions—maybe their capacity for mathematics—tied to a sense of subtle pulls upon their skin--"

"All very exotic. Why is this of interest?"

"They could have had the warp. They could proba-bly—see?--the warp if it were formed anywhere around them—they could tell us things that we just don't know--"

"But—genetics--you say that they had some kind of pat-tern recognition--"

"They seemed to have been largely parthenogenetic. We know they could trade genes—mutually impregnate—some-thing a lot like it, though it was more like attaching a bud, and doing something much like regenerating a limb—but it would drop off, become autonomous—that is how Xenoobsterics advises me--"

"and we would have to uplift them. They never quite got to instrumentality."

"That is correct."

"and you say—you say they seemed to adapt their digestion to different nutritional challenges--"

"They had photosynthesis of a sort, and did not need—could synthesize aminos from basic minerals if they had to—the subtype towards the starward pole seems to have had an aversion to consuming organic nutrition--"

Somethings stirred in Grand Redactor Gates; he lifted up his palm, stretched it across Klufft's capacity for speech.

"They would never have refined crops or done husbandry if they had made the leap themselves. We'd get warp techs but no aid with our current project load here. They'd never uplift. They'd never even refine. They'd have been all over the galaxy doing nothing about what we found instead. They would tweak nothing but our soulless machines, our heaviest burden..."

Klufft shrugged--

Gates stared at him with closing eyes that snapped open of a sudden, as he declared without humor, doubt, pity or much awareness of anything at all, even his own doughy self-importance.

CHAPTER SEVEN

"DAWN"

BY JIMMY EKSTEDT

THE DWARF HELD HIS head in his hands. He shuddered with fear, with shame, with regret for the events that had transpired.

Running his hands through his thick, graying auburn hair and beard, he took a quick glance at his surroundings.

All around him, the halls and passageways of Falkrunn, the subterranean dwarven capital of the Aetherwind Mountains, were dark and cold. Not a soul was to be seen or heard. At least, not a sentient one. The once bustling metropolis was now eerily silent.

Baradin screamed in rage and anguish.

He was War Chief to the king. The burden of responsibility was *his*.

He should've killed the first of those Tyberian merchants that came to peddle their wares. Their gaudy cookware, their silks, whatever unnecessary luxuries that came from Ardos and deeper south.

These men representing the New Dawn Trading Company were scouting out what parts of the mountain they could.

He should've known from the looks in their eyes that they were after the troves of gold that his people possessed, or worse, the Sunstone.

Belwyn.

Baradin thought lovingly of his beautiful daughter, already so skilled at the forge and so beautiful with her lovely blue eyes. She was growing up to be a lovely woman.

He shrieked again in agony as the memory in his mind shifted to the past.

The New Dawn had convinced the avaricious King Tytos to invade the dwarven lands in the Aetherwinds to secure the vast treasures held within. Tytos had raised an army ten thousand strong, with many veteran volunteer soldiers, but just as many conscripts. They marched the hundreds of miles north to fight the dwarves in the southernmost keeps.

Baradin had taken glee in the carnage that ensued. With their superior fortifications and defensive tactics, it was like taking a crossbow to fish in a barrel. His brother, Bardurr, claimed thirty men in the first week of combat alone. They rejoiced in their initial victory.

Two weeks later, Baradin ordered Bardurr to take a company south to attack the Tyberian encampments. After another major victory, repelling the enemy. Bardurr would for the next seven years be the commander of the southern front, haranguing the Tyberian forces and making the conquest of the mountains a living hell for their men.

Baradin choked out a sob. He felt as though his innards were filled with churning wet sand.

Baradin knew something was terribly wrong when one day he heard a mysterious thunder echoing through the mountains. It wasn't magic. The Tyberians couldn't possibly have mustered that many skilled mages.

The [Not sure I follow what you mean here] New Dawn arrived with a second army of ten thousand strong, all armed with some aberration of a weapon he had never seen before.

Lines of riflemen within weeks overran the southern keeps. All contact with his subordinates- Torigg, Garndur, and eventually his brother, went silent.

Bardurr's severed head, right eye socket blown out by a ball round, was sent back to the rear echelon as a warning by the New Dawn with a note of warning. Surrender yourselves into servitude or meet your doom.

They weren't just after the gold.

Baradin pounded the surrounding walls, scrambling on all fours while alternating between shouting and sobbing. He coughed and hacked, trying to expel the mucus from his sinuses.

The dwarves in the southern keeps put up a valiant resistance, killing thousands of Tyberians, but once the experienced, veteran warriors were slain, tens of thousands of his countrymen were enslaved.

"Damn you, damn you, damn you!" Baradin screamed as he bloodied his fists against the polished stone walls of the corridor. Even the dwarf himself couldn't find out if he was more so cursing the New Dawn or himself. Tears running down his eyes, he clumsily zig-zagged down the darkened corridors. He felt as though he was suffocating in the pool of his doubts.

He somehow made his way back to his family's home.

For the first time in a long time, he smiled.

Baradin recalled the hundreds of lively, jubilant meals he would enjoy at his family longhall. The House of Frosthelm had lived in this manor for thousands of years, and even in the near four hundred years that Baradin had lived here, he couldn't think of a single time here that didn't fill him with joy.

The voices of the dead screamed in his mind again. Baradin went wide-eyed as he collapsed to the floor, spasming as he envisioned the events of the recent weeks past.

Around the table, Baradin laughed with merriment as he glanced around. He saw Bardurr, his wife, Iliana, and his sons,

Bheldur, Bendrigg, and Rangrim. His little girl, Belwyn, tugged on his sleeve from behind him. The young lass looked at him with her big blue eyes.

"Papa? Do you want some more ale?" she asked, as she extended a pitcher of the brew her mother had made for this feast.

He paused. *This isn't real.* Baradin knew.

With that, reality came to be as Baradin held the mangled, mummified corpse of his daughter by the smashed long table.

He dropped her suddenly, as the cacophony of a thousand of her screams reverberated inside his skull. He stumbled around his ancestral home, coming across the bodies of his slain family and friends.

Bheldur died out in the southern front, surrounded by Tyberian spearmen and ran through in a dozen directions.

Bendrigg and Rangrim he last saw at the beginning of the assault on the outer doors of Falkrunn. Though in his stupor he had investigated hundreds of corpses throughout the halls, he couldn't discover whether his other sons were amongst the dead or the enslaved.

"You're a coward", the malevolent voice whispered into his brain.

"Damn you!" Baradin shouted as he picked up a tankard and shattered it across the wall.

"You turned and ran the second the Sunstone fell"

Baradin smashed his head into the wall, hoping that Moradin would take his life. The voice was right. He fled the battle.

The Sunstone was a colossal stone, over ten feet tall and five wide. It glowed with a fierce and awe-inspiring magical light. Also, curiously, it vaguely held the shape of a helmeted dwarf's head. The Aetherwind dwarves had worshipped this rock for thousands of years, and they suspended it in the uppermost chamber of Falkrunn, enabling it to illuminate near every space within the vast network of tunnels and passageways. It served as a constant reminder to dwarfkind that even in the darkest of depths, there is a light.

Once the New Dawn got within range of it, they targeted the ceiling of the Sunstone's cavern with artillery and scores of rifle rounds. A stalactite fell from the ceiling and smashed into the idol, cracking it and plummeting it to the ground. It was then that the survivors lost all hope and surrendered.

Baradin ran.

He sprinted through the passageways, trying to find Belwyn and Iliana. He reached the door when he realized there was at least a squad of New Dawn soldiers inside. Baradin barged in with a rage, swinging his axe in a savage arc. He cleaved one soldier through the side of the head, taking the helmet with a piece of skull still inside. The men knew surprise took them and they were at a disadvantage. They quickly backed away to reassess the situation, but Baradin hacked and chopped at the startled soldiers until they had joined the thousands of dead in Falkrunn.

Baradin thought he had finished them all until he heard the screams of his wife and daughter. His blood chilled in a way he had never thought possible, even in the glacial peaks of the mountains. He ran towards the forge room, where he heard their voices. A tall New Dawn swordsman in black armor was standing over the maimed and bloodied forms of Belwyn and Iliana.

He unzipped his trousers.

"Which one of you is going to be the first spoil of war?"

"NO!"

Baradin tackled the man and forced him to the ground. With a vicious salvo of punches, Baradin beat the soldier bloody and nearly unconscious. Grabbing him by the collar, he dragged him and with his bare hands, shoved the face of the repugnant monster into the hot coals of the forge.

The smell of burning flesh filled the room for a few seconds until Baradin shoved the entire body into the coals. He turned around to aid his loved ones.

Belwyn and Iliana had died.

The deafening screams and lamentations of all the dwarves of Falkrunn filled Baradin's mind as he kept about his mad careening around the halls of Falkrunn. The evil doubts in his mind were still louder.

You could've taken the fight to the humans.

You could've fought and died like your sons did.

You're not worthy of your family name.

"I am not worthy of my name", Baradin choked out to himself.

You fled Falkrunn altogether while the New Dawn rounded up the survivors and chained them up for slavery on Iron Island.

When he saw the severed limbs and deep gouges slashed across his wife and daughter's bodies, he ran. A dead sprint into the deepest reaches of the colony, where not even the New Dawn would find him, as he howled and cried for everyone he had lost.

You've been in the ruins for nearly a decade now, and you still don't do a damn thing to save your people.

Baradin saw a tiny glow peeking out from the rubble and sand on the floor. He stopped, having felt the first bit of clarity in weeks. .No. He shuddered. It had been years that he had lingered alone. Tears ran down his cheeks.

He reached out and picked up a tiny fragment of the Sunstone. He raised his hands and shouted,

"I WILL CROSS THE SEA TO SAVE MY PEOPLE!"

Despite the terror that even the mere mention of the sea brings to dwarves, Baradin meant every word of that. There are few things that bring more absolute panic and terror to a dwarf than the prospect of drowning. Most don't have the ability to swim, and they bear no knack for anything aquatic. For the first time since the fall of his people, Baradin had a glimmer of hope. A shred of purpose.

He equipped armor and donned a great sword by the outer gate. Clutching his piece of the Sunstone, he set out into the cold and unforgiving elements, walking towards the sea.

Baradin Seacrosser was going to bring about a new dawn.

CHAPTER EIGHT

"BLAZING SWORD"

BY DAVID OLIVER KLING

SUMMER OF **2022**

Gretchen Merolla slams down on the brakes of her red Volkswagen Jetta while looking up from her cell phone at a red light. A text message from Gretchen's friend Dana states, "R was calling u a cunt yesterday at work." The light turns green, Gretchen hits the gas and looks down at her phone and presses the call button, ringing Dana's phone. She hears the phone ringing through the car's speakers as her phone syncs with the car's wireless system.

"Hey," says Dana, "got your attention?"

Gretchen responds, "Hold on," as she lights a cigarette and takes a deep puff. Continuing with, "Rhoda ain't got no business saying shit about me. Fuck her."

"We need to put the two of you in a room and let you fight it out," says Dana.

Gretchen responds, "I would beat her ass."

Gretchen takes another deep puff from her cigarette and then pounds her car's horn as another driver swerves in front of the Jetta.

"Get off the fuckin road," Gretchen shouts at the driver.

"You trying to rupture my eardrums," says Dana.

"Oh, sorry about that. Some jerk-off just cut me off. People don't know how to drive in this damn town," says Gretchen while taking another deep puff from her cigarette.

"You work'en today?" asks Dana.

"Yeah, 7 to 7. I'll be there, but I hate working nights," responds Gretchen while taking another deep puff on her cigarette. "If Rhoda is working, though, I may have to beat her ass."

Dana laughs and says, "Hopefully, she will be assigned to rehab hall. That'll keep her busy and out of your way."

"I hope it's a slow night. I could use a break," says Gretchen, taking another deep puff off her cigarette.

Gretchen hears a text message notification over the car's wireless speaker system. She looks over at her phone and notices a message come through from her mother.

"Dana, I got'ta go. My mom texted me and I'm sure I'm gonna get yelled at about something. I need to call her, and I'm almost home anyhow," says Gretchen.

"I hear ya. See you at work," says Dana.

Gretchen hangs up the phone, then rolls the window down slightly and flicks her cigarette out the window. She then presses a speed dial on her phone that reads "Mom," and she can hear the phone ring on the car's wireless speaker system.

Gretchen's mother answers the phone, "Gretchen?"

"What's up, mom?" says Gretchen.

"I need you to go to the store. Pick up some milk. We are out and Sammi needs it for her cereal. You might also want to pick up something for lunch," her mother says.

"Okay, mom. Anything else," says Gretchen.

Her mother responds, "No, that's it. See you soon."

Gretchen disconnects the phone and lights another cigarette. She passes the road she would have taken home and drives a half mile to the grocery store where she sits in the parking lot and finishes her cigarette. When finished, she again rolls down her window and flicks her cigarette outside the car onto the grocery store parking lot.

***

A UTUMN OF 1985

A metallic blue, fifteen-year-old Dodge Charger speeds down the road. Driving the car sits a woman in her late twenties. Blond hair, green eyes, with a weathered look that was once what people would call beautiful. A cigarette hangs in her mouth.

In the front passenger seat, a boy of ten sits nervously.

"You know how hard it is to raise two kids?" says the woman, holding the cigarette in her right hand while casually steering the car.

The boy nervously responds, "No. I guess it would be hard. I do okay watching Sam while you're at work, though."

"I should never of had you bastards. What the fuck was I thinking?" says the woman. "Your daddy might still be around if you two were better kids! What was I thinking? I'm an idiot. It makes sense that I would have idiot kids."

"Do you think Daddy will ever come back?" says the boy.

"Fuck no," shouts the woman, as she takes a deep puff on her cigarette. "What do I keep telling you? He ain't never coming back. You and Sam pushed him away from me. He couldn't handle what I deal with every day. He was weak, just like you. You don't listen. You never listen."

She takes another deep puff on her cigarette, which is almost burned down to the butt.

"That's it. You know what to do, put your arm out," says the woman.

"But, mom," whimpers the boy.

"I said put your fucking arm out," shouts the woman.

The boy reluctantly puts his left arm up in a horizontal position, several scars pepper his arm. He looks down at his t-shirt, an image of the cartoon Voltron: Defender of the Universe. The boy clenches his teeth and thinks, *From days of long ago, from uncharted regions of the universe, comes a legend; the legend of Voltron, Defender of the Universe…"*

The woman extinguishes the cigarette on the boy's arm.

The boy feels the pain of the burn rush through his body. His teeth still clenched, he continues to think, *"…a mighty robot, loved by good, feared by evil."*

The woman discards her extinguished cigarette butt out the cracked window, as the boy cradles his arm.

The car speeds down the summer midwestern road. A few minutes later, the woman pulls the car into the parking lot of a Dairy Mart. She opens the door, steps out, turns back, and looks into the car and says, "Stay here, Mommy will be back in a minute." She closes the door.

The boy turns in his seat to face the back seat, wincing from the pain in his arm as he does so. As he looks onto the back seat, driver's side, there sits a young girl of about six. She is crying.

The boy says, "Don't cry. It'll be okay. She'll be back soon, don't cry. It'll be okay. I promise."

The girl nods, trying to compose herself. She wipes away her tears.

After a few minutes, the woman returns to the car.

"My precious little ones, did you miss Mommy? I got you something," the smiling woman says while handing the boy two boxes of candy cigarettes. "Mommy got cigarettes for all three of us. Give one to your sister, Jackson."

The boy takes the candy cigarettes. He puts one on his lap and turns to face the back seat, fighting to hide the pain he feels. The girl reaches out to grab the box of candy cigarettes he is handing to her as the boy says, "Here, Sam."

The woman turns on the car, backs up, and speeds off, saying, "Like Gran'pa used to say, 'smoke 'em if ya got 'em.'"

The woman laughs and starts humming the words to the song "We are the world."

Jackson thinks, *"Form Blazing Sword!"*

***

S PRING OF **2023**

Lieutenant Kyle Dell, support lieutenant with the Massillon, Ohio Police Department, sits at his desk looking at crime scene photos while looking up at one of his three detectives and says, "Blake, how are these cases tied together?"

Detective Glen Blake responds, "That's just it lieutenant. The only thing I... we can figure, is proximity and the way they were all killed."

"Fire," says Dell?

Blake nods and says, "Fire and blunt force trauma. The first two victims, James Sandy and Virginia Sanderson never received an autopsy. Blunt force trauma was never confirmed, but I suspect there were some. Sandy lived just over the county border into Summit County, but Sanderson was local. Arson killed them, and at first, we didn't tie them to the others."

"You three working with Summit County?" says Dell.

"Oh, yeah," says Blake, "It's all above board. We're working with the county guys because we have some more Summit County victims. Sandy isn't the only one."

"How many in total?" asks Dell.

Blake responds, "We have seven victims. Sandy and Sanderson are both white and 52 and 56. Cleveland Boulter is also a white male and 67. Latonia Millon is a 37-year-old black female. Dusty Krask, a 23-year-old white female. Saul Fester is a 70-year-old white male; and Georgia Fissell is a 29-year-old mixed, Asian white female. Sandy, Boulter, and Fester are from Summit County, Fissell lives in Jackson Township, and the rest are from Massillon. Oh, and yes, we're also working with the Jackson Township folks, too."

"Walk me through a typical crime scene," says Dell.

Blake responds, "With Sandy and Sanderson, the entire house burned down, and we later linked them to the rest because we found their bodies near the front door of their homes. The others are similar. For example, we found Krask on her front porch. Her left knee cracked, and her leg took several hits from either a pipe or perhaps a baton. He then splashed her with an accelerant, gasoline for sure, and lit her on fire. The pipe or baton, likely right before or while on fire, hit her in the head. It looks like the perpetrator of these killings takes out a leg, douses the victim and keeps them down while lighting them on fire."

Lieutenant Dell looks through the assorted photos of the various crime scenes and says, "This is gruesome. Right in our back yard. No idea how he selects his victims?"

Blake shakes his head and says, "Like I said, we have nothing except cause of death and proximity. And proximity is nebulous because we have victims in Massillon, Jackson Township, and the south side of Summit County."

"There must be something that ties them all together. They frequent the same businesses, they go to the same church, something." Dell let out a deep sigh and continued, "Looks like we have a serial killer, but targeting random people? That's weird. Keep working the case."

"I'll keep you posted," says Blake.

***

S UMMER OF 2022

A man in his late 40s sits in a Toyota Tacoma, a four-door pickup truck. He watches a woman discard a cigarette out of her car window. He stares at the smoldering cigarette on the pavement until he notices the car door of a red Volkswagen Jetta open, and a woman gets out of the car. He immediately notices her long blond hair. She has an athletic frame and dashes into the grocery store. He thinks about it, and puts her age to be early 20s, and wonders about the color of her eyes.

He waits. Eventually, the woman returns to her car. He watches her stow a bag of groceries in the back seat, get into the car, and exit the parking lot. He turns on his Toyota and follows the Jetta.

He follows her for a half mile until she parks the car in a driveway. The house is pleasant. He doubts it is her home. She is too young to afford it on her own. He watches her get out of the car, collect the groceries from the ack seat, and enter the house through the front door.

The man sits in his truck, now parked at the house next door. He rubs his left forearm up and down, feeling the occasional bump on his skin from old scars. He sits, collecting his thoughts. He knows he doesn't have a lot of time.

The man gets out of his truck. He opens the door to the extended cab of his truck and inside a plastic tote rests several sealed metal cannisters with screw-on lids. He grabs one cannister, and the liquid inside sloshes around. Next to the tote is an extendable baton. He loosens the lid of the cannister and puts the baton in his back right pocket.

He walks up to the house, and knocks on the door. He waits.

He thinks to himself, *"From days of long ago, from uncharted regions of the universe..."*

The door opens.

At the doorway stands a girl of about six years of age. She looks up at the stranger and says, "Hi. I'm Sammi. It's short for Samantha. What's your name?"

The man looks down at the girl. "Nobody. I'm no one. Wrong house," he says.

***

W INTER OF 2042

A woman in her early forties,
with obviously bleach blond hair, wears dark blue nursing scrubs, gets out of
her car, and walks toward the entrance of an assisted living facility, The Inn at Meyers Lake – Canton, Ohio. The parking lot is well lit and the clock in her car reads 10:40 PM.

She is buzzed into the facility;
she walks up to the reception desk. As she approaches the reception desk, a holographic image of a woman appears sitting at the desk followed by the image greeting her in a slightly robotic voice, "Welcome to the Inn at Meyers Lake, a premium assisted living facility designed to make the lives of our residents complete. How may I assist you with your visit?"

"My name is Gretchen Merolla. I'm a nursing assistant with Nurses Calling of Canton. I was told I would be working tonight in memory care," says Gretchen.

The holographic image responds, "Welcome, Gretchen. We have been expecting you and are grateful that you are here to supplement our staffing needs. We have assigned you to our memory care unit, which is in the back of the building. If you turn right, and then left and go to the end of the hallway, you will see the entrance to our five-star memory care unit. The access code to the unit is star-four-three-one. The charge nurse for the facility is Reggie Powers, and he is at the nurse's station to the left. There is one other nursing assistant in memory care tonight and her name is Kara, she can help you with duty assignments. Do you have any questions?"

"No. I'm good," says Gretchen as she walks away towards the memory care unit.

Gretchen walks around the memory care unit for a few minutes, she notices a woman in her twenties leaning against a counter at a kitchenette holding a coffee mug. Walking up to the woman Gretchen says, "Are you Kara?"

"Yeah," says Kara, "I'm so glad you're here."

"Hey, Kara. I'm Gretchen."

"Let me get you up to speed," says Kara as she walks out of the kitchenette and into the main living area of the unit and points down the hall to the right and says, "Your area is everyone from here to the end of the hall. It's easier if we round together. You know how it is, turn and changing is faster with two. We round at 1:00 and 3:00 and start getting them up at 5:00. We get up as many as we can before day shift shows up."

"Works for me," says Gretchen.

"Oh, I almost forgot. There is one resident that still needs put to bed. Let me introduce you to Jack. He doesn't say much, but can be combative," says Kara.

"I'm sure I can handle him," responds Gretchen.

Kara and Gretchen walk down the hallway, passing several resident rooms until coming to a room that has 408 on the door with the resident's name under the room number, Jack

Bridgewaters. They enter the room, and Gretchen notices it is like a shrine to Jackson High School. A large stuffed polar bear lies on a table in the room's corner. A few championship banners hang on the wall. A man in his late sixties sits in a wheelchair, staring at the television.

Two separate old photographs of two different young men rest on the wall, both depicting football players in Jackson High School football uniforms. Pointing to one of the photos, Gretchen says, "Is this him?"

"I think that one is him, the other is his dad. From what I'm told, they both played Jackson football and Jack was named after Jackson Township. As you can see, he was really into it," says Kara.

Jack stares at the television. His eyes glassy. The television drones on...

"*Welcome back to Cold Case Files Exposed.*" An elderly woman appeared on the screen and the caption under her read, "*Retired Massillon Police Detective Regina Little.*"

"*My partner and I, detective Glen Blake, never caught the killer. Eventually, he just stopped killing. We had suspects, but nothing panned out. The only actual link we could find tying the victims together was that they were all smokers and...*"

Kara turns off the television and turns to Jack, "Hey Jack. This is Gretchen. She's going to get you in bed. She and I will check on you tonight, too."

Gretchen stares at a frame mounted on the wall that includes an anchor, stars, and several medals. A small plaque within the frame reads, "Fire Control Technician Master Chief Jackson Bridgewaters, United States Navy." A handwritten note within the frame states, "Bubble Heads forever," and includes several signatures surrounding the saying.

Gretchen says, turning to Jack, "Thank you for your service."

Jack sits there, he stares at the blank television screen.

Kara asks, "You got this?"

"Yeah, I'm good," says Gretchen.

Gretchen pushes Jack back a few feet so she can easily stand in front of him. She bends down so she can look at him face to face. Jack looks up a little and stares into her green eyes. Gretchen says, "Hi Jack, I'm gonna get you ready for bed."

Jack perks up, looks around and sees his cane resting at the end of his bed a couple of feet away from him. He thinks, *"From days of long ago, from uncharted regions of the universe, comes a legend; the legend of Voltron, Defender of the Universe..."*

Gretchen starts looking through Jack's dresser for some clothes to dress him in for bed. Jack continues to eyeball his cane.

"...a mighty robot, loved by good, feared by evil," thinks Jack.

Gretchen turns down Jack's bed.

Jackson shouts, *"Form Blazing Sword!"*

Gretchen spins around just in time to feel a cane make contact with her face.

CHAPTER NINE

"...ON THE HUMAN CONDITION"

BY ANDREW MILLER

N OTE: *THIS ARTICLE WAS originally written (though never yet published) after Terminator Genesys came out; it does not take into account Terminator: Dark Fate, which I have not yet seen. The full title of the essay is "Terminator & Battlestar Galactica and the Human Condition."]*

I love the Terminator Franchise. When I first saw it it scared me to death. It is responsible for my fear of nuclear war (due to that scene in T2 where Los Angeles is destroyed in powerfully well-depicted nuclear explosion) but I love it! I love it because it is action-packed and unabashedly fun, and I love it because I think it can have a deeper point to make; a point similar to that of the 2003 remake of Battlestar Galactica, however I think that the developers of that show were far more conscious of the point being made than the developers of Terminator; more on that below.

A few years ago, I did a Terminator marathon in preparation for seeing Terminator Genesys in theaters, and as with all the Terminator movies, Genesys was fun. I do not think, however, that it added much, if anything, to the franchise. There is enough of the story left open for a sequel if they really wanted to pursue it, but it ends (spoiler alert!) much as Terminator 2 ended: with the theoretical destruction of Skynet and the end of the war against the machines before it begins.

Terminator has been screwed up by its developers, pretty much since Terminator 3: Rise of the Machines. There was hope with Terminator Salvation, but for some reason, it did not do well in Theaters and Critics panned it (not as badly as they panned Genisys). Honestly, I thought they ought to have skipped T3 and gone straight into Terminator Salvation as a Prequel to The original Terminator (1984), and let T2's ending stand; that way the rest of the story could focus on the War with the Machines, rather than a series of car-chase scenes and cool explosions (although admittedly, a series of war films would no-doubt include these as well).

The real missed opportunity with the Terminator Franchise (and with Genisys, I fear they may have missed it permanently) is the opportunity to frankly discuss the human condition as well as humanity's tendency toward self-destruction. Of course there are commentaries in the films about the human condition; such as John Connor and the Terminator's insightful dialogue in T2 where Connor muses, "we're not going to make it... people I mean." To which the Terminator replies "It is in your nature to destroy yourselves." Beyond that, however, most of the discussion of the human condition misses the mark in the sense that humanity is portrayed positively, and machines negatively (except for the Terminator himself who assimilates to humanity).

In T2, a central underlying conflict is between the humanistic child, John Connor, and his mother who has lost touch with her humanity (as a result of raising her child alone in a perpetual state of boot camp, as well as the abuse suffered at the hands of her captors in a state mental hospital), and is hell-bent on stopping Judgment Day, even if she has to act like a machine to do it. John finally reawakens her to her own humanity when he tries to prevent her from killing Miles Dyson.

T3 has little to do with the human condition in an existential sense, and discusses more the concept of fatalism (admittedly a very important topic given Climate Change and other issues resulting from human self-destructiveness). In T3, Judgment Day is inevitable. If Miles Dyson didn't develop Skynet, someone else would have. More on this below.

Terminator Salvation, as good a movie as I think it was, fails in the sense that its commentary on the human condition is much the same as T2, namely that it is ultimately a conflict between those humans who want to fight the machines like machines (General Ashdown) and those (John Connor) who understand that they cannot sacrifice what it means to be human in the name of survival. There is also the question of what makes a person human at all. Marcus Wright chooses to be human in spite of his being a machine. But ultimately, in Terminator Salvation, humanity is good, and the machines are evil, just as in the first three movies.

This is where the Terminator Franchise really misses the Mark (and where the 2003 Battlestar remake hits a homerun). Terminator ultimately fails to have a realistic dialogue about human responsibility for its own destruction in the development of Skynet, it also fails to make any attempt to discuss Skynet's right to exist as a self-aware, arguably sentient entity. It is merely the case that humans are good, and Skynet is bad, and the good guys win because Skynet is destroyed.

As a western orthodox Christian, I see the human condition through the lens of Original Sin. This means, among other things, that while God intends humans to be good, and we are good insofar as we live into this divinely-given essence, the reality of our existence is that evil is prevalent. One of the ways I interpret the story of the Garden of Eden is through the lens of Eastern Orthodoxy which teaches that God always intended the fruit of the Tree of the Knowledge of Good and Evil to be eaten so that humans could grow beyond original innocence, but only when they were ready, and only under God's guidance.

Unfortunately Eve and Adam realized that the fruit was theirs for the taking. They had the technical skill necessary to pick the fruit and eat it. They did not need God's guidance. They could seize the day. This original sin happens every day. It is repeated throughout history in a never-ending, seemingly inescapable cycle of violence and death. Every time our technical abilities and accomplishments exceed our moral maturity, we repeat this sin. One such pivotal moment was nearly eighty years ago on July 16, 1945 when the first ever nuclear weapon was detonated in Trinity Desert.

The result was that humanity was capable of causing its own extinction (indeed we came very close to it on a few occasions during the Cold War). Little did we know that the seeds of our own extinction had been planted nearly two centuries earlier with the beginning of the industrial revolution, which by the mid-to-late twentieth century would be slowly causing Global Warming. By now, it may very-well be too late to stop Climate Change's near-apocalyptic effects. In both of these cases we ate the fruit of the Tree of the Knowledge of Good and Evil... again. Our technical skills and accomplishments, as a species, exceeded our ability to understand and, accept, and manage their consequences.

So, Full Disclosure: I am not a computer nerd, and I do not understand artificial intelligence. Nevertheless, I do know that it is very conceivable to generate a computer that has metacognition (the ability to know itself as a thinking entity) at which point, I would argue (and I am somewhat fluent in philosophy) that what has been created is a person. If I were using the language of Battlestar Galactica, I might say that we have, at that time, created a Cylon.

NPR even did a report back in 2010 on the viability of eventually downloading human consciousness (which works similarly to computer data) into machines to create functional immortality. This may very well be the next great leap forward for which we are morally unprepared. At this point, it could be argued that we will have become gods in our own right, creating life, creating intelligence, creating sentience. In Terminator, humans do this, and yet nothing is said about the moral implications of this. Nothing is said about Skynet's personhood. And finally, nothing is said about the need for humanity itself to change.

As said before, Where Terminator 3: Rise of the Machines gets it right is in its discussion of fatalism: Judgment day cannot be averted, postponed perhaps, but not averted. Skynet is inevitable. If Miles Dyson didn't do it, someone else would have. If the Manhattan Project hadn't have developed the Atomic Bomb, someone else would have. If James Watt wouldn't have developed the Watt Steam Engine, someone else would have. We cannot go back and unmake the Atomic Bomb, or undo industrialization. We cannot take away the knowledge of good and evil, but what we can do is what Adam and Eve failed to do in the garden... take responsibility.

I suspect that if Adam had not blamed his wife, and Eve had not blamed the snake, that if they had just admitted and asked forgiveness, God's response would have been: "well, we have a problem because you cannot take back your knowledge of good and evil, but because of your repentance, I can help you with it, so you can stay in the garden." What is needed is a change in the human heart that begins with owning responsibility for what we, as a species have done with our technical advancement.

In the Terminator Franchise, Judgment day is averted twice, but human beings are never changed. Human beings are merely assumed good. No responsibility is ever taken for having created Skynet, who although a machine, is a person with moral rights. The closest that we come is Miles Dyson in T2, who is profusely apologetic for his role in Skynet's development, but rather than his acceptance of responsibility causing him to think through the moral implications of creating life, he merely assists in that life's destruction. Without this change, without this repentance, T3 is right, and Terminator Genisys is wrong. Judgment Day is inevitable. It cannot be stopped, only postponed.

The Terminator Franchise had the opportunity to comment on ways in which we are bringing about our own Judgment Day through nuclear weapons, unrestricted capitalism, and human-made climate change, and although it comes close in places, it ultimately elects not to do so. Terminator 3 does not take any time to explain or hint that Judgment Day's fatalism is due to human self-destructiveness, it is simply a plot device in the movie (without which the movie wouldn't make sense, since Sarah, John, and the Terminator stopped Judgment Day in T2).

As they say in Battlestar Galactica: "all of this has happened before, and it will all happen again." Industrialization, poverty, war, unrestricted greed, weapons of mass destruction, human-made Global Warming. Lest you think I am just writing a movie review, I think it extremely necessary to heed prophetic warnings that are often hidden within Sci-Fi Fantasy (often quite unintentionally by the authors). Humans are, in real life, caught in a seemingly inescapable cycle of violence and death; it's not just a movie. It's also not unrealistic to imagine that with technological development, this cycle could end up looking somewhat similar to what we find in Terminator or Battlestar Galactica (minus certain plot devices like time travel and cool space battles). So what is to be done?

END NOTES
Contributor Bios

M UCH GRATITUDE AND RESPECT to all who contributed to The Triumvirate Anthology Volume Two.

***

J IMMY EKSTEDT IS A native of Montgomery, OH. Ever a student of biology, he is a graduate of the University of Cincinnati with a Bachelor of Science in Biology, and works as an aquatic biologist for a local fish hatchery. Jimmy is a passionate fish keeper and reptile enthusiast. He also regularly officiates as the "Dungeon Master" for his friends in his home brew Port Dawn world, of which the short story "Dawn" takes place. His other interests include PC gaming, hiking, and fishing. Jimmy proudly serves in the Ohio Navy.

***

R OBERT HENRY IS AN educator, writer, and a Christian apologist, working as a professor of philosophy at Gateway Community and Technical College in Northern Kentucky. He is the author, under the pseudonym Algernon Ged-grave, of several fiction novels and non-fiction titles available on Amazon and Barnes & Noble, including "The Winds that Stir," "The Tear Drop," and "Milton Riggles and the Exceptionally High Wall." He was also a contributor to "The Cud" magazine, the now defunct "Prodigal Son Magazine" where he served as a Bible answer man of sorts, and an academic reviewer of scholarly material on the prolific magazine "Metapsychology Online."

***

NICHOLAS HURST CHANNELS HIS storytelling into being a mediocre table top role playing games DM, but people still keep coming back every week, causing great confusion for everyone involved. Married, loving father of two girls, and his proudest moments not related to his family are remembering to make coffee before work. He can be found mostly hanging out in Battlegroup Valkyrie Discord.

***

DAVID OLIVER KLING LIVES in Massillon, Ohio with his wife, Jacki, and daughter, Vivianne. He originally started publishing "The Triumvirate" in the 1980s and has been a "DIY" or "do it yourself" kind of guy ever since. He has worked as a hospice chaplain since 2013 and adjunct teaches medical ethics at a local college since 2019. He holds degrees in Philosophy, Religious Studies, and a Master of Divinity.

***

A NDREW MILLER IS AN ordained Priest in the Celtic-Rite Old Catholic Church. Andrew enjoys stories, particularly movies and television and much of his writing has been about the theological implications of fictional stories, particularly movies and television. He is one of the founders of New Faith New Media, a Progressive Faith-Based Media Organization, and co-hosts the Podcasts "A Pastor and a Priest Walk Into a Movie Theater," "Blessed Lunatics," and NFNM's upcoming Youtube show "Philosophy Notes."

***

B ENJAMIN NORMAN PIERCE IS professional dishwasher with BA's in Philosophy, History, and English. He lived in Sophia, Bulgaria for two and a half years, teaching history at First English Language Gymnasium of Sophia, participating in the expatriate writing circles there, and taking time to learn painting. He practices Hermetic magick. He paints in tempera and draws in chalk or pastels, and does some work in purely digital media as well. He self-published a novel, "Snuck Past Death and Sleep," and has an album of Lovecraft-inspired ambient music,"Al-Azif", and a later electronica album, "Three Hooks" available on Spotify, Bandcamp and SoundCloud. He has published graphics and poetry in various journals. He has lived in Madison co-op houses, since 1989. He was an enthusiastic participant in the 2011 occupation of the Wisconsin state capitol building. He is a regular participant in Open Mike Nights and displays art in small galleries and coffee houses. He is a recent cancer survivor.

***

MIR **PLEMMONS** IS A presbyter in the Ecumenical Catholic Communion, a Novice of the Order of Ecumenical Franciscans though a Franciscan of 29 years and has served many groups as a chaplain of 35 years. He's not sure he can identify when he first realized he was a geek! He and his wife live *almost* far enough from Seattle to enjoy his beloved trees and ravines, and he teaches high school special education. He does disaster mental health as a Field Traumatologist when he can. He has extensively taught socioemotional skills, at pretty much every level. He writes and edits in his summers and off time, and both serves and advocates for Intersex, QUILTBAG+, and Science Fiction / Fantasy Fandom. He holds volunteer positions in all the above, plus the Society for Creative Anachronism...oh, and more boring places like the Okanogan Fire Protection District 12.

***

KERRY **PURDY** IS A Boston girl living in Columbus, OH who loves thinking outside of the box. Currently majoring in English at the Ohio State University, in her spare time she loves long distance running and hiking, dark yoga, and writing bizarre stories. She wants to see a world where neurodiversity is accepted and embraced!

***

ROB **STONE** SCRIBBLES TO himself usually. A lover of prose, of Poe, all things Gothic, dark, and forbidding. He typically writes about New England where he grew up because of the thick history and oddities. Many horrors and cryptic stories can be found there. Writing short stories and yet to be released horror or fantasy novels, Rob enjoys the music of the

70's to 90's as his background to accompany his mechanical keyboard that used to be a Royal typewriter.

POST SCRIPT

By David Oliver Kling

As I write this, at 0105 in the wee hours of the morning, I'm listening to "New Age" music that came out in 1986, "Shadow Dancer," by Eric Tingstad. I have memories of listening to "New Age" music that I discovered through Columbia House, the service where you could get up to fifteen cassettes free with your membership. I'm not listening to a cassette this time around. I found the music on Spotify, which I am listening to on my laptop sitting in my living room. The date that I write this happens to be June 16th, 2022. It's my birthday and I am fifty two years old. A lot has happened in that fifty two years. I'd like to say that I have a good fifty two more years, but that would make me one hundred and four and I'm not sure that will happen.

This is a reflective time and I look back at the past and smile, while thinking about the present and how a lot has changed while some things remain the same. Things like a good story or familiar music. Take the time to appreciate what you have and keep an eye on the future. My hope is that in the future my daughter will pick up a copy of The Triumvirate and smile and think, "My dad produced that," and be proud of her father. As I look around my laptop I can see her sleeping and I hope she has a long and fulfilling life.

I hope that you, the reader, finds enjoyment in this Volume of The Triumvirate and that it has brought you some joy. Producing 'zines and other content is a joy of mine and as long as I have content to share I will continue to produce this and other anthologies. Many blessing to you, reader. I'm going to try to get some more sleep.

CALL FOR SUBMISSIONS

The Triumvirate Anthology: A Quarterly of Science Fiction, Fantasy, and Horror is always looking for submissions of short stories and serialized novellas. We accept all subgenres in these three genres of fiction. We accept adult content, but no erotica. Authors retain all rights to their stories; we accept previously published work and reserve the right to republish material already published in The Triumvirate Anthology into an annual anthology. As of this volume we are unable to pay for submissions, but that may change in the future. Please send all submissions to: david.oliver.kling@gmail.com in the subject line put: Triumvirate Anthology Submission.